Hard Times

Also by Darrel Sparkman

Tyler's Road: An Anthology of Western Stories

The Apocalypse Chronicles

Shepherd's Fire

Blood Justice

Broken Arrow

Shepherd's Sword

Chrysalis

After the Fall

Coble Bray Series

Hallowed Ground

Hard Times

A Coble Bray Western Mystery
Book 2

Darrel Sparkman

WOLFPACK
PUBLISHING
— EST 2013 —

Hard Times

Chapter One

COBLE BRAY RODE INTO HARD TIMES A TROUBLED man with nothing behind him but pain and suffering. Men had stood before him—murderers who maimed and killed. Sometimes they came in bunches. The job given to him was to bring them to justice or leave them where they lay. There was no middle ground. He gave no quarter and expected none in return.

The friars from the mission school he'd attended, who gave him their brand of learning, called him fraught with luck to have survived his childhood, but withheld grace. Though they had teachers who'd been over a good part of the world, they feared the fire of captivity by the Apache had tempered his soul into something they couldn't understand. Schoolyard fights against boys much older rarely lasted more than a few moments, and he never lost. The harder it got, the dirtier he fought. The teachers needed the money, or they would have tossed him out.

His was a fine line to walk—the line between hunter and hunted seemed blurred at times. He took no satisfaction from bringing someone to justice or for killing them when forced. For the most part, he believed their sins were his own.

He shrugged his shoulders, feeling the weight of his twenty-five years tighten like a cloak, aging him by a couple of decades. The knights of old drove their broadswords into the soil—the hilt making a cross to kneel before. Like them, the armor of his soul became dented and tarnished.

The town he rode into was a haphazard collection of buildings in eastern Kansas, a few miles west of Joplin, Missouri. A windmill graced the center of the street, blades turning a lazy circle—too dirty to reflect light, its shadow blinked cadence on the trough below. A malevolent sun beat down on his bleached hat, and the pommel of his saddle burned, too hot to touch. Dust rose from each footfall of his horse, following him in a cloud that no amount of speed could outrun.

There was a piece of shade next to an eatery called Jenny's Café, so after a bit of water at the communal well, he left the horse leaning on the building. The manner of the horse reflected the man—too tired to go another step. He moved under the awning and used his hat to dust off his pants and desert-style moccasins that came up to his knees.

After being in the blinding sun, he paused a

moment inside the door, adjusting to the shaded interior. It was a welcome relief and he felt some energy returning. He sat at a table next to the window. A couple of men paused to look, dismissing him as they sipped coffee from blue-speckled pewter cups.

A woman stepped from the kitchen, looking as weathered as the building. She tried to be friendly, he'd give her that. The smile on her face was genuine, and her voice so rough it hurt to listen. As a reflex, he cleared his throat and hoped she didn't notice.

"Howdy. I'm Jenny, and I own this place. I'd give you a menu, but it wouldn't do no good. We got beef and beans, and some fried spuds on the side. A little bread to sop it up with. That suit you?"

Between dried sweat and an ominous mood, his face felt wooden. He hadn't smiled in a while but tried to give her one. "Sounds about perfect, ma'am. Add a tall glass of water and some coffee to that and we're in business."

Her gaze dropped to the star on his vest. "You a marshal?" She glanced to the side as someone dropped their cup, and then turned back with a smirk as the room emptied out.

She looked pointedly at him. "You're mighty fast with that shooter. Next time, put that star in your pocket so you don't make the miscreants around here nervous. We're mighty close to the Nation."

He didn't remember drawing his pistol, startled by the noise of the dropped cup. His smile was slight as he slid the pistol back into the belly holster. "Sorry."

Jenny looked to be a down-to-earth country woman. He liked her, and it was good advice. The Bible says the wicked will flee when no one is chasing them. He reckoned that was true. Except sometimes they don't run. Many a marshal gets killed minding their own business by men who are afraid of discovery or capture. The irony of that did not escape him.

"Next time, I'll do that very thing."

She went to the kitchen. He sat and stared out the dirty window. There wasn't much to see except a few horses tied to the hitch rail in front of a saloon across the street. A rider walked his horse down the middle of that thoroughfare as Coble's mind traveled the back-trails that led him here.

He didn't know if his education was a blessing or curse. He was a youngster and only child when the Apache wiped out his family—old enough to remember his name—not old enough to know why they attacked. There's always a reason. Most of what he remembered about their place came to him later. His folks had a little two-by-twice farm when the Indians attacked, and the fight was over before he knew what was going on. He didn't remember any shooting. Years later, he could figure what happened to his ma, but by the time he figured that out, captivity had hardened his soul. Riding by the old place once, all he saw was scrub brush and rocks, and little else. He remembered wondering why ordinary people put their lives at risk for something of such low return.

He was in his sixth season with the Apache when a cavalry unit attacked the village, led by a scout named McGill. The man took him in and tried to civilize him. In the following years, Caleb taught him everything he could. He left the army and turned into a good sheriff for a few towns. Coble helped and learned what he could from him. No matter where they were, town or trail, he could not neglect reading and numbers. Like many folks, the Bible was the only book they had.

School was one thing Caleb wouldn't let him slack on. There was a mission school run by Franciscan friars for the Indians. He enrolled Coble and then left for a while. Most of their Order lived in the Southwest, and he never knew how this mission came to Kansas.

One day, McGill showed up with a judge in tow and handed him a badge. He told Coble it was time to do some good in the world. Because of his background, it wasn't long before he traveled into Indian Territory serving warrants. McGill went his own way and they'd meet up occasionally in Kansas City or Joplin. Last he heard, the sheriff was in southern Missouri—a place called Big Springs, looking to retire.

Jolted off the memory trail, he flinched when Jenny set food in front of him. Deciding a plate that full needed side-boards or cleaned up real fast, he set to the task.

She stood staring at him, wiping her hands on her apron. "You starving?"

He glanced up at her, swigging some scalding coffee. "No, ma'am. I ate a couple days ago. I'm just getting reacquainted with my appetite."

Clearing her voice, she spoke again. "I've seen you before, you know. It's been three-four years, but I remember."

He gave her a glance but didn't stop with his task of cleaning that plate.

She kept at it. "Why do people call you Deacon? You don't look like no Bible thumper. I been to church in my younger days. We had preachers and elders. Never heard of a deacon."

He took time to swallow his food and take a sip of water. "Look. I can't help what people say. But to answer your question, preachers preach. Elders look after the flock. A deacon is a teacher." He glanced at her. "I claim none of that."

"Still don't answer the question?"

"Some say I chase sinners and read to them from the Book, teach them the error of their ways."

She shook her head and smiled. It washed years from her face. "Well they got that wrong. From what I hear, you mostly read over them at the burying." Her gaze held him a moment. "You don't look like the killer you're supposed to be."

"You're mighty curious."

"Sorry. It's a small town and not many strangers pass through. At least, not interesting ones."

He stared at his half-empty plate, not sure how

to answer. "It's not a mantle I ever took on purpose. It comes with the job. I'm no better or worse than others. It's just that...sometimes a road doesn't go where you want or finish where you expect." He looked up at her. "You just can't see over that next hill."

She watched him eat a moment. "So, did they deserve it—those you've read to from the Book?"

He shook his head and met her level gaze. "A much wiser man than me once said that we all deserve it—one time or another. I expect he was right."

The twinkle in her eyes told him she was about to lay some more country wisdom on him when the sound of three muffled gunshots interrupted their conversation. The shots were evenly spaced and sounded like target shooting.

His handful of spoon and taters paused on its journey.

Her eyes painted the door with an anxious glance. "Maybe it's just a cow pusher drunk on skull-buster." Her voice was skeptical.

A woman screamed from down the street, followed by the sound of hoof beats fading away. He gave a sad look at his half-finished meal.

Sticking a last spoonful of spuds in his mouth, he tossed a dollar on the table. When she went digging for change, he waved her away. He grabbed his hat and stepped outside. A man rushing by with a pistol drawn about ran him over. Seeing a star flash on the man's shirt, he figured the runner was the town marshal. Why he was in such a hurry was a mystery. That shooter was long gone.

Coble paused and looked back. Jenny stood in the door of the café, nervously wiping her hands on her apron. He wondered if that was a habit. She was younger than she looked at first glance and seemed wise beyond her years. Maybe she was like him, putting up a front to guard the one within.

———

THE STAGE OFFICE was a few doors away, with a coach and team tethered in front. If they didn't water those horses soon, they'd drop in their traces. By the time he got there, the marshal was coming out the door with a gray-haired woman in tow. She stood on the porch while the marshal gazed down the street. A faint dust cloud still hung in the air.

He watched the man's gaze look him over and settle on his vest. He could see the man's shoulders slump when he saw it was a deputy US Marshal's badge. The relief on his face was obvious as the man nodded to him and held out his hand.

"I'm Ed Stone, the town marshal."

He shook the weathered hand with some curiosity. This was Ed's town, his shooting—there were things he should be doing, not socializing.

"Coble Bray. Pleased to meet you."

The man stepped back. "Heard of you. You're the Deacon?"

He nodded, waiting the man out. Any passerby

could read the thoughts bouncing around the town marshal's brain by his facial expressions. His gaze wavered between the older woman and Coble. What he didn't expect was the level of honesty.

Ed shook his head. "That man's heading toward the Nation." His glance at Coble wasn't weak... exactly. "I could go after him, but he's already out of my jurisdiction. He killed three good men. To tell the truth, I'm afraid. I know I can't match that man with my gun and doubt he'll come back if I ask polite."

The marshal dropped his gaze and then met Coble's with a pleading expression. "I got a wife and kids."

Coble wondered if this was the worst thing that had ever happened in this tired-looking town as he put his hand on the man's shoulder and nodded. It was a good trade and expected. Most would figure the loss of another deputy marshal wasn't much to write home about. He also knew a man with a family should not take chances.

The town marshal gestured toward the woman. "Mrs. Peabody saw the whole thing." He couldn't leave quick enough. Mumbling something about an undertaker, his run-down boots stomped back the way he'd come.

Dressed in a blue calico with a bonnet to match, with laced black shoes, Mrs. Peabody gazed at him with a stern look through little round spectacles. She reminded him of every spinster school teacher he'd seen or heard about. It was surprising when a slow smile graced her face. He knew what she saw—a tall young man in faded clothes with two pistols strapped to his waist and a bone-handled skinning knife on his left side. His hat had seen better days.

Her voice sounded younger than what he supposed her years to be. He seemed to be making a habit of miscalculating age.

"You going to fetch that boy?"

He looked at her a moment and then inclined his head. "I reckon so." He grinned at her. "You the one that screamed?"

She gave an unladylike snort. "That was the gal inside behind the counter. I swear it was worse than the gunshots—like to busted my eardrums. Then she caught the vapors and fainted. I wished she'd fainted first."

He looked at her a moment, realizing this was a woman who'd been up the river a few times. It didn't make her a bad person, just not a damsel who would ever be in distress. "Do you know who did this? A name, maybe?"

She shook her head. "Seen him around some. I never heard a name, so I just called him Baby Face. He always looked harmless."

He thought of that a moment while looking at someone's leg sticking out the door. It twitched once and then was still. The window was open and powder smoke still drifted out of the room.

She picked up on her story. "Craziest thing I ever saw. Crazy as in strange. That boy walked in the door...nobody paid him no mind—didn't say boo to anyone. He just pulled his shooter and killed the agent, stage driver, and guard. It was like he'd gone to the dry goods store and was pointing out things he wanted. This one...this one...and that one. No expression at all. It spooked the hell out of me—pardon my French. The guard had already unlocked the strong box, so he flipped the lid open and took a bag of money."

She looked at him, shaking her head. "Just one bag, like it was all he needed. Any outlaw worth his salt would take the whole box. Don't make sense."

"No, ma'am. It never does." He shrugged, wondering how the expression on the face of a killer shocked her more than the shooting. Raised on powder smoke?

"So, the best description we have is I'm looking for a baby-faced man who kills casual-like, and with no name."

He started to leave when she stopped him. "There is one more thing."

"Seems like there always is."

She stepped briskly to the hitching rail a few feet behind the stage, the hard heels of her shoes rapping on the boardwalk. "This is where he tied up his pony. It was small, a brown and white paint—kind of looked like my calico cat. Not big like that ugly cuss you rode in on."

He hoped his horse didn't hear her. Old Red was cranky enough without hurting his feelings. "You notice a lot, don't you?"

She shrugged and grinned at him. "Got nothing better to do."

He walked over and looked at the dusty earth by that empty hitch rail. The horse hadn't been there long enough to scuff up the dirt much. It looked as if the right front hoof had a broken horseshoe that hadn't worked loose yet.

————

HIS OWN HORSE acted hungover when he woke him up. Leading him to the water trough, he let him drink a moment—just not enough to swell up. As he settled in the saddle, Jenny brought out a bag and a wooden canteen with a cork in the top. It was an unexpected charity and he was speechless for a moment.

"You didn't get to finish your meal so I threw together some chicken. It's good, cold or hot." She shaded her eyes with one hand and gave him a serious look. "You be careful, Deacon."

He thanked her and rode out of town, tipping his hat to Mrs. Peabody standing sentinel on the boardwalk. What kind of life had she led...that the killing of men bothered her less than the mystery of expression?

Later that afternoon, he stepped off his horse under the shadow of a live oak. Trees and brush choked the banks of a meandering stream, and from a distance, it looked like a green snake that wandered through the rolling countryside of eastern

Kansas. Since it flowed south, he figured it would connect with the Neosho River in Indian Territory. He took a slow look around before examining the churned earth.

Someone drove a small herd of cattle across the shallow water earlier and it took him a moment to find the right tracks. Standing with the reins of the horse in his hands, he studied the trail. The print was there. The trail of Baby Face lay on top of the others, and it was fresh.

He stepped past that oak, leading his horse. Shucking his Winchester from the saddle scabbard, he started a winding path downstream, looking for any sign. The water at the crossing was clear and didn't show any fresh tracks. The fast-moving water of the riffle smoothed tracks over quickly.

As he followed the creek south, his head was up and looking around. He'd see the trail easy enough if it was there. Raised by the Apache as a young boy taught him many things. One was the value of ambush, and this was the country for it. He didn't like anything about this, and it was getting worse with each step. The feeling of being watched rode his shoulders like a sack of rocks. The only sounds were the hoof falls of his horse and the gurgling of water over rocks.

There was a bend in the stream just ahead and he stopped, staying concealed in the brush. A man squatted in the clearing ahead, his pony ground-tied behind him. He held a gun pointed down and he was looking the other way.

The sandy earth was soft so Coble got within a few feet before the man heard something. He whirled and stood as their eyes met. The man didn't bring the pistol up, so Coble didn't dust him off with his long gun. They stared a moment at each other while the ground-tied horse sidled away a few steps.

The pony was a paint, and the man surely looked like a baby-faced boy. Coble figured he was the shooter from Hard Times. Another body lay at his feet and it didn't help his case.

"I'd appreciate it if you'd holster that pistol—real slow." He didn't want him to drop it—a dropped pistol can go off, and you never know what direction it will shoot.

The young man gave in easy, and that was a surprise, if he was the killer. But a shootout would get him dead in a hurry and he'd know that. He figured the man would bide his time, thinking to catch his captor unaware. Contrary to that thought, the boy seemed listless, like he'd given up.

Coble walked behind him, leaned the Winchester against a log, and then grabbed him by the collar, taking his pistol from its holster. "Now back up from that body and kneel down."

He stared at the body as he backed up a few paces with his prisoner in tow. The killer's knees locked for a moment in protest and then he knelt. A quick look around revealed no one else. Coble was nervous about this and looked to see if the man had help. What happened at the stage station was a stone-cold killing. When he looked into the boy's eyes, all he saw was sadness.

"Why did you kill this man?"

"Didn't. That's my pa. He was waiting for me to get back." He nodded toward the body. "Did you look at him?"

Dead men were no mystery to Coble, so he hadn't given the body more than a cursory glance. Taking some rawhide strings from his saddlebags, he tied the boy's legs above his boots and then his hands. "Did you kill those men back in town?"

A tear cut a dusty trail down his cheek as he shrugged. "I did."

"Why kill them? You could have just taken the money."

"We knew the sheriff wouldn't chase me. Those three were the only ones that might. Pa said to make sure no one followed me." He nodded at the body. "Look at him."

The man lay on the ground with his hands folded across his stomach. He may as well have been lying in a coffin. Far as he could see, there wasn't a mark on the body. A pistol was in his holster with the thong over the hammer. If this was the boy's father, he'd either got sick and died, or there was another killer about. He didn't like that thought much, and the feeling of being watched came back to haunt him.

He nudged the body and it was stiff. "When did you last see him?"

"Early this morning, about sunup."

He knew it took less than half a day for rigor to set in, especially in the heat. It would be gone tomorrow.

"Did he know you were going to rob the stage office?"

"He sent me. We needed money. He told me to not take it all. Maybe folks wouldn't be so mad and chase after me." He pointed with his chin over his shoulder. "We got a place south of here."

"Any more family?"

He hesitated a moment. "No."

Coble sighed at that. It might be true, but likely not. They wouldn't be the first to ride away from a homestead and not come back. It was a tough land. He felt sorry for those left behind to continue the struggle.

The dead man's eyes were open and he tried to close them. It didn't work, but he noticed something protruding from his mouth. Curious, he pried the jaw open and took it out. It was something he'd seen a lot. A small cross, like you'd wear on a string around your neck.

He looked around, studying the trees and low hills. A person of reason would figure the man died shortly after the son left. He'd have to accept that premise for now. Few people would stick a cross in their mouth if they were dying of natural causes or have the time. He took the man by the shoulder and rolled him over. No blood or wounds. What killed him? And who? It was what every lawman hates. A mystery.

If he was one of those new-fangled doctors from back East, maybe he could figure out more. He'd seen his share of the dead, some by his own hand. This was different.

He started to get a blanket off the boy's bedroll when something occurred to him, and he gestured toward the body. "What kind of horse did he ride?"

The man staring at the body didn't respond for a moment. "Same as mine. We raised them."

Walking a slow circle, he didn't see any tracks he couldn't explain. No footprints—someone had to lay the body out like that. No tracks, but it was a windy day. It was like he fell out of the sky. He started to look up before he caught himself.

He'd pulled the shell belt and holster from the dead man to add to the kid's gear hanging from his pommel. The bag of gold coins was in his saddlebag. He retrieved a small shovel from his pack that he used for digging a fire pit on occasion. He tossed it to Baby Face and told him to dig.

The ground was soft to about three feet down— that was all the body was going to get. He didn't have a pick-axe to break through the hard pan below. Not the best place for a grave, but he wasn't going to wait a day for the body to loosen up enough to throw across a horse.

Rolling the man in a blanket, they dragged him into the grave and then stood at each end. Coble looked at the covered body. How do you send your son on a mission of robbery and murder? Why didn't he do it himself? Another mystery. He took a worn Bible from his saddlebags, but no verse came to mind for easing the pain of this baby-faced killer. He held the Bible but didn't open it. All things considered, the boy would join his father soon enough. If the judge didn't hang him, the people of Hard Times would.

Finally, he shrugged. "He was your pa. Whatever he was meant to be—what troubles he had...are long gone now. You can take some comfort in that."

His tear-streaked face turned to Coble. "Can you say some words over him?"

Coble nodded with a sigh and prayed for lost souls. As he spoke, his mind was full of that blurred line between the hunter and the hunted. The prayer was short, and he didn't know if the boy was pleased —nor did he care. Everyone makes choices. He made his.

Something splattered his face, and the only sound he heard was the boy falling on top of his father. He dove into the nearby brush with a fleeting glance toward the rifle leaning against an old log. He had a strange thought that if all this flotsam came from high water—it must have been before he was born. It was dry and hot.

What wind there was blew away to the north, and he figured that shot came from a long way off. He wasn't surprised he'd not heard the shot with the wind blowing toward the shooter. Since no more shots came, he wondered if whoever made that shot didn't want him. The mysteries were piling up.

He stood, half expecting a bullet, and walked to

the grave. It was a head shot to the boy, and from the angle and direction, the shooter had to be in a low line of hills about a half mile away. Coble knew he couldn't make that shot in his wildest dreams. He'd heard of sharpshooters during the late attrition between the states doing it. Even at his best, he'd have to see something before he could shoot at it.

As he watched, a rider appeared on the crest of a hill. They stared at each other across the distance and he couldn't tell if it was a man or woman. Finally, the shooter raised a rifle over head for a moment, shook it, and then disappeared from the skyline.

He could have leaped in the saddle and given chase. He glanced back at the open grave. There were two men that needed burying, but more important, he had a tired horse. He gave a disgusted sigh and the sorrel pricked up his ears. He'd check for tracks later but didn't have much hope of finding anything. He wasn't too sure if what he'd seen was any more than an apparition, but the kid's head wound was real enough. Maybe he just wanted it to be his imagination, to assuage his guilt for not giving chase.

———

AFTER ANOTHER HALF HOUR, the burying was over. He made a poor job if it. Two men in a shallow grave with a lot of extra soil piled on top. There was nothing on either of them to say who they were. If anyone came asking, he'd send them here.

After watering the horses, dusting his clothes, and washing away the grime from his hands, he rested on a log, eating the chicken Jenny sent along. She was right, it was good cold. If the water in the stream ever rose this high again, it would wash the bodies out of that shallow grave. He looked at the cloudless sky. Pigs would be flying by then.

He packed up and caught the reins of the kid's horse. Mounted, he sat and studied the hills. He had the cross the killer stuck in the older man's mouth... at least, he assumed the killer did it. A cold-blooded murderer was getting away free for the moment. With the same honesty the town marshal gave him —he admitted to himself that he was afraid.

Moving to the top of the hill where he'd last seen the rider, he looked back and could see the fresh grave. If this shooter wanted him dead, it would have happened. Maybe he should take comfort in that, but it didn't set well.

A fluttering of white caught his eye and he rode down the back-side of the hill to find a piece of paper stuck on a small branch. There was a printed note on it.

"You are too soft. If you don't harden up, you'll never catch me."

He crushed that paper into a ball and started to throw it away. On second thought, he smoothed it out, folded it, and put it in his shirt pocket. Was this a game?

He figured he was a fair to good tracker. Not as good as the Apache who'd taught him, but close. A quick look around revealed no dust trails, so the killer was probably walking his horse—or sitting somewhere waiting for Coble to ride by. There was a slight indentation of a trail on the dirt surrounding the bush. It didn't take much to figure out they'd tied burlap on the hooves of the horse, so any tracks would be gone soon. As if making the point, the wind picked up in gusts that threatened to unseat his hat and was starting to smooth over the dusty soil. The shooter couldn't keep the hoof-covers on long, but it would be enough to hide a trail. Then he'd be looking for a nameless person, riding in an unknown direction with no trail or guiding information. The definition of a fool's errand.

With a sigh, he turned back toward Hard Times to give a report to the town marshal and return the stolen money. Three men gone in a day for no other reason than desperation. Two others were dead at the whim of an unknown assailant. And none by his own hand. That was an irony he could not escape.

The lengthening shadows caught his attention. It was getting late, but he could make it back for supper.

The shooter? Coble would bide his time and keep his eyes open. Whoever made that shot might think this was a game. The taunting note was an invitation to play. He would not.

The worst part, if anything was worse than

death, was not knowing—and he was sure that's what the killer wanted. Why kill the two men—father and son? Were they on the way to kill the man's family? Or, take over their homestead or ranch—console the wife? Why?

No answers came to him as he followed a long-eared jackrabbit bouncing along the trail into heat-waves making the horizon a shimmering mosaic.

Chapter Two

COBLE BRAY SAT ON THE PORCH OF HIS RANCH house in eastern Kansas, his boots propped on the rail in front of him. A couple of rose bushes planted next to the porch were having a poor time staying alive. Between the beetles and the heat, there wasn't much left. In the fall, he intended to transplant a few young trees, but they'd need rain to moisten the parched ground.

He could hear his new wife Maria humming as she puttered around inside. His thoughts wandered as he gave contented scrutiny to his surroundings.

A year had passed since he buried a baby-faced killer and his father in a shallow grave. There'd hardly been a day he hadn't thought about it. Even when he'd been in Big Springs looking for a killer of little girls, not a day passed that he didn't think of the murder in Hard Times. He considered it a failure that he hadn't chased down the man who'd killed the boy and his father. It still rankled him.

His gaze picked up a trail of dust moving toward the sanctuary of their home. It was a hot day in August of 1878 with no wind to give relief. The dust stood like an arrow pointing toward them and had an ominous look. It was too much for the time and place, and they'd had few visitors. Not that they weren't in settled country. It's people he had little trust in—an attitude often returned in kind.

When he stood to step inside, Maria appeared and handed him the old brass spy-glass kept in his saddlebag. When he telescoped it out and looked through, he could see one rider and something large in a buggy. He pulled out his handkerchief, cleaned the lenses of the glass, and looked again. The figure riding the horse looked familiar. An odd configuration, considering. It was a long, uncomfortable ride from anywhere in a buggy.

She didn't say anything, her expression curious as she handed out his Winchester. They'd met and had a whirlwind courtship in Big Springs when he'd gone there to help a friend. It was a caution how the more they learned of each other, the less they spoke. She seemed to learn and anticipate his every whim, no matter how mundane. Like most men he'd known, it was hard for him to express his feelings, but she seemed to know that and took that in stride.

One of his fears was that she would grow tired of the mundane ranch living and walk away. She'd seemed edgy lately, often staring at the horizon, lost in thought. When he asked, she'd just shrug and not give an answer. He hoped she wasn't pining for better things somewhere—imagined or not. Maybe the new had worn off and she was examining the dusty, worn face of their union. For his part, he loved the peace and tranquility. With a past known for gun battles and high tension, he loved the quiet. And he loved her.

Pete Santos was her father, his friend, and saddle partner on a lot of trails. He took a bullet while helping at Big Springs. Unknown to Pete at the time, his daughter had forgone the schooling he'd paid for because it was too boring. Maybe there was a lesson in that. Long before they met, she'd taken a job for the Pinkerton Agency. When Coble found out, he insisted she stop that damned quick. Pinks had a short life span west of the Mississippi.

Regardless, he felt she had his back if needed. Her matching rifle would be leaning just inside the door close to hand. His Winchester had the long barrel, hers was the shorter saddle gun. It didn't matter. She was a damned fine shot with either one.

When the riders drew close, he put the glass on them again. She came up behind him with her hand on his back, hair smelling of lilac soap and freshness. There was a question in her gaze.

"It's Priest—and a stranger."

She shaded her eyes with her free hand...a strange gesture under the shady porch, and then looked at him. "This can't be good."

His longtime friend was a Lutheran minister. He called him Priest to vex him and was moderately successful. Dressed in black, Priest was riding a big black mare. He wondered if the man regretted his choice of color on such a hot day.

The stranger following in the buggy was too big to ride a horse. Not fat, just the biggest man he'd seen...ever.

When they stopped in front of the veranda, their resident vaquero seemed to pop up out of thin air to take care of the horses. An older man, tough as sun-dried leather, he'd showed up one day saying Pete sent him. Coble didn't argue—except to explain to him they were land rich and horse poor. He'd shrugged and disappeared into the barn. He rarely showed up for meals, and they didn't see him much. But if Coble lifted his hand to do something, he'd lay it on the back of his vaquero when he put it down. He vowed to watch close someday to see how he did that. It reminded him of one of those leprechauns in Irish stories, seeming to appear from nowhere. Although a soft-spoken man, something in the vaquero's eyes spoke of stories better left untold.

They stood waiting, calm as only the uninformed can be. He hardly recognized Priest, another man with a strange past—though he'd never hear it from him. Pastor August Schuler always dressed in black, but the only vestments he wore today were tied-down pistols and a skinning knife. If he came with a story, it wouldn't be a good one.

Coble finger-tapped his own collar. "I guess you're not here to minister my tarnished soul?"

Priest stepped up to the porch and they shook hands. He moved on to hug Maria before his voice came over his shoulder. "I'm afraid I had to give up that quest." He smiled as she kissed him on the cheek. "The mantle of your soul was too much to bear."

They turned in unison as the buggy squeaked and lurched. The occupant seemed to get taller as he stepped off. "You men sound like a couple of Methodists looking to wear a cassock."

The giant didn't need to step up to the porch to be at eye-level. Smiling, he held out his hand to Maria. "My name is Judge Colin MacGregor. I'm here to enlist your husband."

She gave a very unladylike snort. "Then you've made a long ride for nothing. He's promised to give all that up."

Coble's voice was conciliatory. "Maria, let's hear them out."

Her head and gaze jerked toward him so fast he was afraid she'd break her neck. Her eyes went soft a moment as she searched his face. "No. Please don't do this."

Opinions came fast for Maria. She looked at the hand extended in friendship, gave the judge a look that scorched the earth he stood on, and then turned and left. Not before ripping Coble's thin cotton shirt and leaving a scratch down his back that would need salve by the next day. His flinch and painful grunt died as he watched her walk away. She was not a gentle soul.

The judge looked at Priest. "That didn't go well."

Coble tried to put his hand on his back. "Well, you've had a long ride. Whatever your mission—the answer is no. But it's a hot day. It's cooler inside if you want to make your case." He looked askance at the judge. "Although, I'm not sure where you'll sit."

Priest stepped through the doorway, and Coble could hear him trying to quell the sudden anger consuming his wife. The pastor might get burned in that process, and he smiled at the thought. When mad, Maria could fry eggs on her forehead.

The judge spied a sturdy bench on the porch and grabbed it with one hand. "This will do."

Arms held wide in invitation, Coble ushered him and his bench inside and watched him duck under the door frame. He lost a bet with himself on that one, figuring the giant would crack his noggin.

After moving a chair and replacing it with the judge's temporary throne, they gathered around the table. Things took an unexpected turn when his suddenly domesticated wife placed large pewter mugs of coffee in front of everyone and then sat in demure repose with a gentle smile. She watched him so intently he felt like a cat's toy waiting for the paw to drop. Coble vowed not to drink from his cup until after the other men—and he'd watch them carefully for signs of discomfort.

He could understand her anger, just not the degree of it.

They looked at each other, waiting for someone to speak. Like throwing a skunk through the church door at Sunday service, the judge opened the game by placing a US Marshal's badge at the center of the table. He'd pinned it to a beautiful, hand-tooled black leather holder that would fit in a shirt pocket. It lay there reflecting a dull light from the windows and seemed to project a life of its own. Coble couldn't decide on the degree of malignance it represented.

Maria stared at him with eyes black as the coffee she'd poured, her face drained of color. No one could hold the anger she was showing without something popping loose. It was a side to her he'd not seen.

Priest laid a hand on her arm and she glanced at him. She wouldn't take that kind of casual contact from just anyone. He tried to calm her. "Maria, it can't hurt to listen."

Coble watched all this with a curious detachment, holding his wounded back away from the chair. "What's this all about?"

Judge MacGregor pointed to the badge. "That is yours and you deserve it. That pompous ass in Big Springs took it away from you unfairly. If you sign these papers, they return your badge as a special appointment whether you choose the responsibility or not. Only the president can revoke it. Consider it a reward for services rendered."

"A reward or penalty?" Consequences occurred to him as his fingers twitched, wanting to reach for it...until Maria asked the obvious—something his muddled mind hadn't approached.

Her voice was hoarse. "Why? Why now? Why would you do this to us?"

Priest picked up the thread of thought. "We have more murders."

"We?" Coble's glance was quick, but he decided to let that part of it go. "What's new? We're on the edge of Indian Territory. It's a lawless place, and every wannabe bad man is drawn to it. Thirty miles to the south is Joplin, Murphysburg, or whatever they decide to call it. That whole place is becoming the new Sodom and Gomorrah west of the Big Muddy. They have more gambling halls and bawdy houses than outhouses. The mines are spitting out zinc and lead, and money is pouring in. It will only get worse."

He paused to let that sink in. "There's nothing new in killings. Nearly as many deputy marshals have died in the Indian Territory as murderers hung by Judge Parker. Hell, it wasn't too many years ago eight deputies died at the Goingsnake massacre. Few men around here live to old age."

The judge nodded. "All that is true. But these killings are different and I've taken an interest in them."

"Different than just plain old murder?"

They watched him like some carnival attraction. He wouldn't have been surprised if they'd poked him with a stick just to see what he'd do. The clock sitting on the mantel ticked through the silence as he watched them for some clue to their real purpose.

He fought against asking, knowing it was a path he shouldn't take—one glance at Maria told him that. She was alternating between sadness and hot anger. The star in the center of the table seemed to edge closer to his hand of its own volition before he withdrew his elbows and folded his hands in his lap. The dull, reflected light winked at him.

His gaze took in Maria, eyes glistening as she stared at him. Though her head shook, she never lost contact with his eyes. He'd never met anyone who could live in his mind so thoroughly, seeming to examine his every thought before handing it back to him in better shape than received. That could not be good for her sanity.

Priest had that cold-eyed smile as he watched the byplay between them. He'd been a pastor for as long as Coble had known him. He always wondered if it was a bad career choice because, as a man of God, he still drew a line between killing and murder. Many of the clergy did not agree.

He looked back at the judge and, with a long sigh, gave in. "How different?"

A muffled sob erupted from Maria as she stood and walked away. Her arms clutched around herself making her back rigid as oak lumber. She looked to be losing a battle within herself—a fight he'd precipitated. He didn't know how to take the words back and wasn't sure he wanted to. Looking at her, he knew she'd taken his interest in the killings as a physical blow of defeat.

Judge MacGregor inclined his head toward

Maria. "My apologies. I didn't mean to upset her. Perhaps I was too abrupt. May I speak freely or should we go outside?"

Coble's gaze settled on his wife. "There's no need for private conversation. Understand this. Maria played a big part in catching the killer of those girls in Big Springs, whether Judge Johnstone liked it or not." He turned to look at Judge MacGregor. "My wife is upset but is no innocent, and she's strong." His smile was grim, flexing his back. "She can hold her own."

"As you wish." The judge cleared his throat. "Like you said, we are no strangers to death and other sorts of mayhem in this part of the country. But for the most part, it's between outlaws, their own element and the law, or men cheating in a game of chance—the occasional bank robbery and or drunken brawl. I'm sure you've dealt with this."

The judge continued. "The good people, or I should say the common folk, are largely isolated from this. Businessmen, farmers, ranchers, all manner of people that don't frequent that side of mankind seldom see a killing. The normal cowman carries a gun for varmints and self-protection if needed. Few people in larger towns carry guns anymore. They rely on people like you for protection. I run into people every day who believe violence is not acceptable. Unless, of course, it is used to protect them."

"That may be true in the bigger towns. Not out here." Coble's voice was so bitter he surprised himself. "So, us bad folk are killing each other off? In your learned opinion, is there a downside to that?"

The judge looked at him for a moment and looked surprised. "The downside? Someone is preying on common people...the innocent. And they are thumbing their nose at the law."

He watched the judge a moment before replying. "I was told by a killer of young girls that there are no innocents, only those that claim it. So, again. How does this concern me? You have a lot of marshals at your disposal."

Judge MacGregor glanced at Priest, seeming to stall for time, and gave the impression he wasn't on steady ground. "You come highly recommended. Your set of skills are different than normal. As the population grows and pushes farther west, we're seeing a different kind of murder. The use of the telegraph is spreading, and it helps lawmen talk to one another and share information."

"What we're finding is a type of killer who is rarely caught. We hear of them—see the results, but then they fade back into society and disappear. Some are women, poisoning their victims or using other methods. Some are men, as you've found out. Their choice of victims are always the helpless and unknowing. I could list ten or twelve that have been caught in the last few years—we estimate most have not."

With his gaze on the badge, Coble struggled to pay attention and idly wondered if Maria slipped something in his coffee. The judge's voice was just background noise. He could hear him mentioning names—Doyle from Detroit, a Whetstone from Saint Louis, Pomeroy...killing children, husbands, and indentured in new and inventive ways. None meant anything to him and he struggled to see relevance.

Maria didn't look at him as she walked back to the table to plead his case. He wondered if she thought him inadequate to do it himself, or unwilling. "Why Coble? It sounds like you have a handle on the situation. As a judge, you're in a good position to pull people together. You don't need him."

Coble nodded to her. "She's right. I've given up the quest of justice. After all, we've been married but a month. We're just getting to know each other." His smile brought a brief one of her own. "Something we should have done earlier, no doubt. But we're making up for lost time. Truth is, I don't have an interest in your problems. My pointing out the killer in Big Springs was luck and a gut feeling, not some kind of magical power. Plus, there was no conviction."

The judge sat up straight on his groaning bench. "I don't give a damn about convictions and less than a whit about how the job gets done. There is someone working in this area. I want them found. I want them stopped. I'm told you're the best for the job. It's as simple as that."

Shaking his head, Coble was starting to argue

when the judge interrupted. "August? You should tell him."

Priest started as if woken from a dream. For an unguarded moment, his haunted expression and hard, angry eyes marred his features. He ran a hand over his face. "I never told you, but I was seeing a lady. It wasn't all the time, but often enough. She'd come for supplies to Kansas City and stop in to the church at odd times. It reminded me of your schedule. She was more handsome than pretty but a gentle soul of rare insight. I loved talking to her and intended to ask her to be my wife."

He looked at Coble, eyes red with unshed tears. "She was a good woman."

Maria tried to put her arm around him but he shrugged her away. Stepping back and a little shocked, she looked at her husband and shook her head.

The sadness in Priest's voice hit them like vinegar on an open wound. "She was murdered."

Coble shook his head and was unable to speak for a moment. Words are inadequate in the face of anger and more than useless in times of sorrow. He knew Maria would be more qualified to handle this if Priest would let her. He'd often wondered if Priest had any interest in women in general, and his shrugging away of Maria seemed to fortify that notion.

"I'm sorry, my friend."

Priest shrugged. "It wasn't your problem." His gaze lifted to Coble. "She knew you."

"Me?"

"She knew Coble?" Maria's gaze swiveled between the two of them. She must have been surprised there was part of his mind she hadn't explored. "How?"

Priest's voice was surer, showing his usual control. "Remember passing through a town called Hard Times? She ran a small café there. When we talked of you, she told me her impression of you was of a haunted soul but a good man. I agreed."

Coble searched for a name but couldn't come up with one. The only thing he remembered about that town was the killings he'd found there.

"Her name was Jenny Slocum."

The name and face came back to him then, though he'd never heard her last name. He remembered thinking she was homely, yet wise in her advice given freely to a lonely man passing through.

"She was murdered?"

Priest nodded. "That's why I took off the collar. Wanting revenge, I could no longer give nor receive communion. And then I killed a man. My sermons of peace and reconciliation to the congregants seemed a bit hypocritical afterward."

Coble nodded, still wondering what the problem was. "I'm sorry you felt the need to quit the ministry. But it's not all bad. No man should get away with a killing like that."

"See that you remember those words." His gaze was feverish and held a plea for understanding. "I killed the wrong man." He shrugged. "Oh, it was justified. When I realized he wasn't her killer, I tried to walk away with apologies. The man tried to back-shoot me. There were witnesses that cleared me." He shrugged again in the manner of a tired man trying to work sore muscles. "You might say he had a farmer's hands and a disposition for other things besides gun work."

Understanding everything placed before him was like watching a Ghost Dancer weaving in the moonlight—vague and uncertain. "Why did you think he was her killer?"

"A passerby that I didn't know mentioned a man had bragged on it. He thought I should know. My anger kept me from realizing the stranger had to be told to come to me by someone."

Coble's next question slipped out unbidden. At this point, he didn't know what difference it would make. "How did she die?"

Priest's gaze never wavered. "When found, she was lying on her bed like she'd gone to sleep—hands folded over her stomach. Those who saw her thought she'd just up and died for no reason. No sign of struggle or wounds."

They'd known each other a good while, and Coble was still digging to find the source of his friend's haunted expression. "There's something else."

Priest nodded, glancing at the judge. "There was a cross stuck in her mouth, and a key stuck between her fingers. I figured the cross was to disrespect me." His voice turned hard. "To disrespect God."

"What kind of key?"

His friend glanced up at him with a startled look. The cross was the most important item to Priest, and it was obvious the key hadn't brought a lot of thought.

"It was like a big hotel key with a bit of pink ribbon on it. It could have been hers for all we know. Why?"

"Just wondering. If someone is leaving bits and baubles for clues, my question is, why? And a key to what? It doesn't make sense."

When he glanced at Maria, she was staring intently at him, hands covering her mouth, eyes impossibly large. He remembered she'd gotten the story of the baby-faced killer from him on a warm night of sharing experiences and communal thought. With her memory, she wouldn't have forgotten a word of the tale.

He thought a moment while they watched him. He didn't often get to correct his friend. "You're wrong, Priest. It's doubtful your occupation had anything to do with it at all. I'm guessing, but my thoughts are that you and poor Jenny were a convenience. Jenny because we both knew her. You because we're friends and would bring the story to me. The second cross is to tie her death to the previous one."

Another thought occurred to him. "Which begs a question."

His confusion mirrored on all their faces, except Maria. Her ruddy complexion had lost a fair amount of color as she sat with her eyes closed. That she was acting odd crossed his mind. He thought she was praying. If so, he might join her. The road he was stepping on had an end of hazy uncertainty.

"Who would know all these things?"

He rose and walked to the mantle over the fireplace. A small box held the only evidence he had of the other killing. It had haunted him since and he thought of it often. He'd been afraid then, and it was a feeling he didn't like. He was afraid now, but in a different way. Not a fear of injury or dying—he'd made that peace with himself long ago, but of something he couldn't understand. How do you fix something with no start and an unclear finish?

Setting the box on the table, he opened it and took out the small cross, careful to handle it by the top. The bottom had a small brown smudge on it that he reasoned might be poison. It was the only thing that made sense.

Priest sighed as he carefully pulled a cross from his pocket and laid it by Coble's. They were similar in make, cut from soft metal. His voice seemed like a rasp on wood. "There's more to tell."

Coble gave him a sad smile. "There always is."

He pulled a small piece of paper from his pocket. Smoothing it out, turning it so Coble could read it.

"Tell Deacon."

He stared at the writing on that note a moment. If it was the same person, he'd expect more subtlety. Why tell him now like he was late to some game? Were they impatient? Was this someone he'd slighted in the past? He pulled out the paper from his box, compared the two, and showed it to Priest.

"You are too soft. If you don't harden up, you will never catch me."

He shook his head, finger-tapping the paper, and a wave of sadness pulled at his face. "I never tried to find this one. Things came up. The easier path was to forget it and I had warrants to serve. It's my fault. I'm sorry, Priest."

Priest watched him like he was a puzzle he'd not seen before. "Sorry? How do you figure?"

Coble's thoughts were back in Hard Times and of a tired horse and lack of a trail. "I should have tried to follow him. But the shooter killed a man who'd surely hang for murder at the first opportunity, and it was more a mystery than immediate hardship. If I'd reacted different, not shirked my duty, maybe this wouldn't have happened. Jenny would still be alive. I should have tried."

Nodding, Priest's gaze bored into Coble's eyes. "You can remedy that."

The judge sat like a giant hawk perched on a limb and watching the oddities of man playing out under him. He'd started things in motion. Now he seemed to be watching how the drama would play out. Coble was still surprised the house wasn't leaning in the judge's direction just from his bulk.

"May I see the key?" When it lay by the cross, Maria gasped. She sat with tears coursing her cheeks, unwilling to meet Coble's gaze. Her hand was a fist that beat cadence on her thigh...slow and gentle, but still a fist. He was positive she knew his decision already and couldn't believe that was a healthy ability for her. This was a rift that would be hard to repair.

Coble looked at his friend. "What's your reasoning? You know the cost to both of us. Are we seeking justice, or am I simply the horse you ride to get revenge for Jenny?"

Priest shifted in his chair. "You once accused me of speaking in riddles. Now it's turnabout." He shook his head and shrugged. "Is there a real difference? One serves the other."

Coble's gaze slid from Priest to his wife. He didn't know if she could see the remorse he felt, though she seemed to journey through his mind at will. That was an indignity he wished she was spared.

The badge seemed to burn his palm when he picked it up. "Then to answer your original question...I shall."

Chapter Three

AFTER COBLE SIGNED THE JUDGE'S PAPERS AND took the oath of office, they strode outside. He watched Maria standing out by the corrals. The vaquero appeared with the visitor's horses. It took him a few moments to harness the buggy and cinch up Priest's saddle.

The judge reached out and shook his hand. "I take it you wish us to leave?"

He hadn't said a word, but once again, the vaquero had read his mind. "It would be better. You're only a couple hours from places that can put you up for the night. It seems I have a marriage to repair."

Priest walked to his horse, glancing at Maria's rigid form. "Sure you don't want me to stay? It would be a poor start to your renewed career if you were hurt on the first day."

Coble smiled at him—a smile he didn't feel like

giving. "That would only result in both of us being flayed. This won't be a pretty sight."

His nod was a grimace of pity. "Then where shall we meet?"

"Hard Times is west of Joplin and south of here. One murder occurred there. That was Jenny's home, so that's two murders tied to it. I don't believe in coincidence. It's a place to start. I'll meet you at the café in a couple of days, if it's still there. If not, I'll be around. It may be a dead end, so keep your eyes and ears open. I'm at a loss for other possibilities right now."

Priest stepped into his saddle but seemed to hesitate. "Coble..."

He held up his hand. "Don't back track now. You and the judge brought this to me. I accepted. Actions have consequences for all of us."

His gaze locked on Maria. "We'll just have to live with it."

"Coble?"

"There's more?" He'd never seen his friend appear so uneasy.

"Do you still pray?"

Startled, he looked at his friend a moment. "Every day, but it's hard. I'm still looking for that absolution I'll never have."

Priest sighed and slumped in the saddle. "I cannot. I gave up my collar, killed a man in anger, and now...I cannot."

Looking at his friend, the irony of the role

reversal didn't escape him. How many times had he gone to the Priest's church seeking answers?

"We are tarnished knights, my friend. That's a fact. It's hard to know the right or wrong of it. Every person we meet thinks they have God on their side. The late conflict was a good example of that—the North and South fighting under God's banner. Sometimes I think God has retired to a tropical home, leaving us to our own misfortunes. I wouldn't blame Him."

Coble continued. "Be patient. It'll come to you. That's not something you misplace like your lucky dollar. It'll come."

"I think not. For the first time, I'm afraid, Coble. I fear we'll become what we fight against."

———

THE TWO MEN rode away with the buckboard clattering and creaking under its load and Priest glancing back often. Coble approached Maria with measured steps as she leaned against the poles of the corral. The sun was behind them, and her face was in shadow, putting golden highlights in her dark hair. She'd taken a quirt off the post, and he watched that leather idly slapping against her thigh with some trepidation. Her voice was low and full of sadness—and anger.

"How could you? Dammit, Coble. We're practically on our honeymoon."

He leaned against the rails. "I didn't feel I had a

choice. You were there, same as me. All the reasons were laid out for both of us to hear."

Her glance at him was quick. "Reasons that made sense to you, not me. I'm left to fend for myself. What made you decide? Was it hearing of that woman's death?"

His answer was slow in coming, but he'd never lied to her. And he wasn't sure his reasoning would take scrutiny.

"If there are innocents, she was one. Her being of interest to Priest made it personal and possibly the only reason she died. I value my friends. He asked for my help."

"But you don't your wife?" Her sigh was more of a sob. "I've seen the scars on your body and heard you say you'd give it up. You promised. What happened? There are always killings. People die. It's the way of the world."

"You get one chance," she continued. "Stay with me—or we can go someplace where we can live in peace. We cannot do that here."

"I gave my word."

She caught his gaze with a watery stare. "What good is your word? You gave it to me and now you've broken faith in a way I can't take."

He shrugged, having nothing to say and not liking the bitterness in her voice. He didn't have a good answer—at least, none she'd like. He'd hoped for more understanding.

Her voice kept beating on him. "If you couldn't give it up, you could have done like Sheriff McGill.

Pick a small, peaceful town to live in. But, no. You had to agree to do this? Try and find some sick, cold-blooded murderer?"

"It's no different than before. And McGill died anyway, for all his peaceful intentions. Besides, I'm thinking this murderer has found me. It will do no good to run away."

"Don't downplay this like you can't help yourself. No one forced you to take the job. How many more wounds can you take? And you're wrong about this one. I feel it. This will be bad." She studied his face. "You don't see it, do you? You think this is just another puzzle to solve."

He shrugged, reaching for her. "It can't be any worse than what we've gone through before. We're partners, aren't we? Help me figure it out. Come with me."

Her head-shake was so violent he feared she would injure herself. "No. Not on this. I'm scared, Coble. I won't be with you. I will not go through this again." Her tear-stained face was a contrast to her defiant eyes. "No woman wants to see her man riding off to chase people who kill with no more feeling than stepping on a bug."

"If not me, then...?"

"Oh, spare me." She gripped his arm, staring at him. "If you love me...you'll stay."

From her expression, he realized this was her last stand. His chest felt hollow. "And if you love me, you'll come with me. Your place is at my side. There's nothing holding us here. We've not had time to make it a home or put down roots. The vaquero can take care of things."

Her hand dropped limp to her side. "Priest is right...you talk in riddles. Listen to me. If you go...I won't be here if you happen to make it back. And I do mean if."

Anger, ambushed by panic at her words, coursed its way through him. "I don't understand. Maybe you'd better explain that to me."

"I'm leaving. I don't know where I'll go or what I'll do. I took care of myself years before we met and I can do it again. But I'll not wait for you to return in the back of a buckboard with a crazy man's cross stuck in your mouth. I...will...not."

He reached for her but she stepped away. How had it come to this? She'd become the anchor in his small world and was out of control. It startled him, but he realized what the crazy killer wanted may already be happening. A creation of fear and chaos.

"Maria, don't do this. You're my wife."

The tip of her quirt slashed across his cheek, leaving a thin line of blood. She whirled on him, screaming, "We were going to have babies. You promised."

It's a strange feeling to be married to several different women at once. They all looked the same, at least on the outside. She'd had fits of anger before, but nothing like this. Now, he wasn't sure which woman stood before him, or which he wanted back. You can't pick and choose—this one I want, this one I do not.

His face burned and blood trickled down his face as he watched her march back to the house. He wondered why he kept shooting himself in the foot of life...for reasons that tear and strain logic? Did he have a brooding soul that could not stand happiness? But if stupidity was the shirt he wore, he could not easily change it.

The door slammed and he hoped it wasn't permanent. At least he couldn't hear her nailing it shut. One misbegotten decision might cost him a wife, and the one thing that would fix it—was something he couldn't do. Go back on his word. The irony didn't escape him that he'd already done it with her. How do you hold your honor high in one hand for all to see and yet let it go with the other? That was a politician's trick.

Not liking himself much, he started back toward the house, hoping her anger was subsiding. A window opened next to the door and his bedroll flew out to land rolling in the dust, followed by saddlebags and a canteen. His pistol belts dropped onto the porch, and he saw her brown arm gingerly lean his Winchester against the sill. It was misplaced caution because the rifle fell over when the window slammed shut.

His sigh was a labored thing as he began picking up his belongings. He had them all in hand when the door opened and she stalked out with a bag, heels thumping on the porch. She dropped it on top of the pile cradled in his arms.

"Maria. Talk to me. Please."

"Shut up. You're dead to me. I won't come to your funeral—if you get one." She hesitated a moment and then reached up and touched the cut on his face, wiping the blood on her shirt. Her voice went from anger through tenderness and ended in anguish. "I'm sorry I can't be what you need. I'm so sorry."

Alarm ran through him at her tone. It occurred to him they were both sorry yet pursuing their course anyway. The door slammed again and he took a step toward it before stopping. To what end? Maybe some time apart would cool things off. And he intended to come back alive.

His nose dropped toward the bag. It had opened slightly and he could see bread and meat. And an apple. He didn't know they had apples. If his investigative skills were so poor he couldn't find an apple in his own house, how could he find a killer?

The answer came to him as it had once before. The killer had found him. All he had to do was survive.

He gazed at the door, not knowing what to do. He could see her vague outline through the window, shoulder's shaking as she wrapped her arms around herself—a job he should be doing.

Never one to coin a pretty phrase, he still reckoned himself a reasonably smart man. Sometimes slow to react and long to ponder. He'd read once that moods of mind may be a disease of thought at the expense of intellect. What bothered him most was that he knew what that phrase meant. If the friars had created a monster in him, it was that he read too much...and thought of the meaning in the words and phrases that told a story with words said and unsaid.

If he truly spoke in riddles as she said, then she was the enigma that wrapped his soul—the mystery he couldn't fathom. Could she, in her volatile nature, both love and hate him? Was she the ex-Pinkerton agent full of fire and tough as nails, or a simple woman wanting hearth and home and babies to raise? Which mood of hers was kind enough to give him food for his journey? She may be crazy as a loon, but then he'd been accused of the same thing with far more reason. Self-reflection could only make him sigh and shake his head.

Standing in the dust before their house, his mind worried over the last few months. She'd staked him out for her own. Lassoed him and pulled him in. But even with that, he bore equal responsibility for that capture. He feared they took the yoke too soon, not knowing each other—what drove them. Time would tell that tale.

Like her or not, he'd understood the widow in Big Springs. She was easy to read, giving the choice of following, or not. That luxury escaped him with Maria.

Hoof beats receded from the barn as he looked around. A horse cantered across the field and seemed packed for a trip. Much as he'd appeared, the vaquero was leaving in a cloud of dust...the one who always knew what needed to be fixed before

Coble could lay his hand on it. He hoped this wasn't an omen.

He turned away and saddled the paint, strapping on the bedroll and saddle bags. The Winchester went into the saddle boot. Starting to loop his pistol belts over the saddle horn, he stopped. With slumped shoulders and fumbling hands, he fastened the belts around his waist, checking the loads and letting the hammers down on empty chambers. Girded for battle and starting his knightly quest with trepidation and a weary soul. Alone.

———

COBLE COLD-CAMPED THAT night after putting a few miles between him and a volcano named Maria. He'd looked often over his shoulder for signs she'd burned the house and outbuildings. He understood her anger, just not the ferocity of it. What underlying problem triggered that explosion? Pride wouldn't let him admit it might be him.

When he stopped under a cottonwood, next to a small stream, it was just him and the sack lunch—and a field rat so persistent he thought he'd have to shoot it. He finally rewarded the rodent with a bit of bread and meat, watched with a smile before he tasted his own meal. The rat didn't die, so he felt reasonably safe eating his cold supper.

She'd tossed him out of their home in anger. He could understand that, knowing her temper. To give him food to start his journey was beyond his understanding.

————

THAT DAMNED KEY! Maria cursed under her breath as she walked to the corral. Clutching her stomach, she took a couple of deep breaths to calm down, but that didn't help the sweat popping out with cold chills. She'd put the ribbon on it herself. The ribbon came from her own dress, cut with a borrowed knife, tied to the loop in the key, and given to a man as an act of faith so he could visit her anytime.

There were two messages sent this day. The cross was a token of death. She understood that one all too well. The key? A message.

She thought that part of her life was gone but realized she'd been fooling herself. Gazing at the empty corrals and surrounding grassland barren of cattle or horses, she knew what she missed—and what she thought she could give up. The key could only mean one thing. Something that had happened a long time ago, and thought safely buried, had come to life. It was coming for her and tied with murder. She ran a shaky hand through her hair, reaching for water to slake her sudden thirst.

Her thoughts drifted back to New Orleans. Coble thought her work with the Pinkerton's was just office duties and she let him think that. She let them all think that. An acceptable lie. Starting at a tender age when her father thought her safely enrolled in boarding school, she found herself good at getting information from men. Sometimes from the women next to the men in question. It became a thirst for her. The hunt. The seduction. The end game. Leaving one to start another. Changing her looks, her identity. It turned into an addiction far worse than Coble's quest for justice.

Then came the wide-open town of New Orleans. There was no vice, no peculiarity that you couldn't find there. Her target was Oxford Graham, a gambler well known with the upper crust of society. His dealings in the underbelly of that city caused the interest. He had information the Pinks wanted on contraband shipments. Playing the part of a displaced southern lady down on her luck, it was easy for her to get next to him. She got the information after a few weeks. And she got him. Another notch on her belt.

But she'd seen him kill. Where she expected anger, all she saw was a cat playing with a mouse. It was horrifying and, for some reason, disappointing to realize he drew more satisfaction from taking a life than being in the arms of a woman—it was a drug to him more powerful than opium.

She got away from him as fast as she could, thankful to be alive. A few weeks later, she found out the information passed to her was useless, fed to her by a master. He'd known what she was doing all the time. He'd put her notch on his belt, and people died because of it. And then he'd disappeared.

It was after that adventure that she realized

being a whore for a detective agency wasn't fun anymore. They didn't care how she got information —just that she got it. And she was well paid. That fact stopped her cold. Well paid. A whore.

She envied Coble's single-minded purpose. Most thought him a brutal gunman showing little mercy. But she knew his lack of guile was a front he put up while his mind evaluated the problems before him. He was not a simple man. If you dress the part, people will think you're an educated and smart person. Dressed in range clothes and run-down boots? Nothing special.

But better than most, she knew the risks before him. Some gunmen put notches on their pistol grips for the men they'd killed. Coble's notches were on his soul, peeling it away in pieces and chunks. She could only watch and pray he'd stop.

But what now? Coble didn't know of her real past. Couldn't know. He'd leave her if he found his adventuresome wife had a past more sordid than he could imagine.

It was decision time. She could make up with Coble later. But Oxford Graham could blow it all up. She had to see him and had manufactured the excuse to do it. Mad at him, she would go to Kansas City and talk to Priest if he was still there. While doing that, she'd have to find Oxford Graham.

One thing she knew. The man from New Orleans was equally as dangerous as Coble. In some ways, more so. By his own admission, Coble was not subtle. And this killer was. A smile and pat on the back would simply get him close enough to put a knife between your ribs.

If the killer from New Orleans was after her, for whatever reason, she needed to protect her husband. He would not understand this kind of man. She loved Coble. But she knew she couldn't be what he imagined her to be. If Oxford did the cross-killings, she'd find out. Maybe she could get close to him and be the one holding the knife

Chapter Four

Coble sat his horse on a low hill overlooking Hard Times, Kansas. As if he and the paint weren't uncomfortable enough, rain shattered the hot August drought by rain pounding them like a hammer on an anvil. The problem with prairie soil is that a little water goes a long way, and it was coming down in buckets, turning the earth to soup nearly hock deep on the horse.

The mid-afternoon sun hid behind roiling clouds to leave their part of the world in near darkness. Lightning flashed to show the way down the hill, the resounding thump coming a second later. He didn't need the light, he could follow the river of water. Any military expert might call their position on the hill untenable.

He'd seen a cow hit by lightning once. The remains looked like it'd swallowed a bomb. Anxious to vacate high ground, they floundered down the hill and cut a foot-deep trail in the mud.

From what he could see, the town had grown. He was coming in on the main street—the only street when he'd been there before. Highlighted by continuous lightning, the original buildings still looked tired and weathered in the rain. A loose shutter banged cadence in the wind. The windmill was still in the middle of the street, blades locked and peppered with bullet holes and dents. He hoped that wasn't an epitaph for the town.

Another line of buildings spread perpendicular to the old town and that street pointed east toward Joplin. The brightly colored paint on the new buildings wouldn't last a year—possibly longer than the businesses themselves. The amount of buildings that appeared in a year's time was a testament to entrepreneurs, no matter which side of the law they called home.

Behind the garish walls with their false fronts and second-story banisters stood a couple of tent cities of sorts. It was an assortment of abandoned wagons, shacks made of pilfered lumber, and army-style tents left over from the war. Some of the tents were blowing away, leaving their soaked tenants to give chase.

Experience told him if there was trouble in the town, it would come from people living in these. Considering new businesses to be the herd, the denizens of the tent cities would be the wolves patrolling around the edge, feeding on the unwary and weak.

An alley between buildings lit up with a couple

of flashes, close to the ground. Against the rain and wind, he heard no gunshots. He figured some miscreant had called down their own version of lightning and a soul was forfeit. It wasn't his problem. He wondered who the town marshal might be.

Jenny's Café was where he'd left it, sporting a new sign hanging from the awning. Someone worked at lighting lanterns inside, the light casting shadows against the windows. He reined in at the front rail. His paint wasn't too happy with that choice.

Still...he'd had Maria's sack lunch for supper last night and hadn't eaten today. Married life with someone trying hard to please had him used to regular meals. Was he soft already? And when did they stop trying? How could he get so complacent in a month's time? How had it gone to hell in those short moments, lacking decision and reason?

It was hard to get his head around her response. Her unsettled nature surprised him. Things were good when they agreed. Once they did not, they lost their path in anger. Maybe that was just life. How we handle anger paves the road we travel. The coat of indecision was starting to get comfortable. It weighed heavy on his shoulders and he didn't like that.

A hired enforcer for an over-reaching cattleman once told Coble, "My reasons for living are not yours, and what I hold as honor is not yours."

He felt the enforcer was correct in his opinion and no amount of discourse would change it. The political discord that cost so many lives in the War Between the States made that point painfully obvious. Before and after. People of divergent thought rarely come together, often ignoring any gesture of understanding from others.

To prove the point, the enforcer, after telling his philosophy with studied eloquence—tried to kill him. The gunman seemed to be a thoughtful and articulate person, someone Coble would like to have known better. Unfortunately, the amount of time between eloquent thought and palming his pistol got the man killed. He was quick of wit, but slow of hands.

Coble was worried about leaving Maria alone, not that she'd given him much choice. But he knew his vaquero was pounding the trail toward Pete's place. He figured within a day they'd be riding to help her—or coming for his hide. He wouldn't lay odds on either decision.

His memory of the eatery wasn't perfect. It didn't seem much had changed inside. He sat at a table by the window. There must be some sort of plan laid out for building a place to eat. Most looked the same, inside and out.

From the lack of customers, he wondered how the place stayed open, or if bad food drove people away. While he watched, oily smoke gathered close to the ceiling and spread to the corners of the room. Finished with his job of firing up a few lamps, a man came over and handed Coble a menu.

This was new. It was strange that he remembered Jenny telling him a menu was a waste of paper. All they had was beef and beans, with some bread to sop it up. The new management added apple pie—guess it took paper for that.

The man spoke while wiping his hands on a rag. "Welcome, mister. Passing through? Haven't seen you before."

He was a short, stocky man wearing a white shirt with an apron around his waist. A pot on his cook stove must have exploded and the apron took the blow. It appeared he visited a barber often and didn't seem to be Coble's idea of a cook. But Coble needed information, and the talkative man suited his purpose.

Coble's soaked and battered hat dropped to the table with a wet thump and he leaned back in the chair. "The way the town looks to have grown, I'd think everyone is a stranger around here."

The man shrugged and nodded. "You have a point. Some call it progress but it split the town in two. In this part, we're acquainted with just about everyone. This is the old town. New folk mostly visit the other side. It's more exciting with the gambling halls and such. They're open every hour of the day. Why, we even have an opera house with ballroom dancing." His smile grew. "Right next to a bawdy house."

"Do the doves charge extra for dancing?"

He just stared, making no comment.

It sounded interesting, dancing girls and bawdy

houses and all, although right now, a good meal sounded better. Peace and quiet suited his mood.

"I rode through here a while back and met Jenny. Someone told me she died. Did you buy the place from her?"

The man looked at him a long moment. "Didn't have to. I'm her husband. Or...was."

Coble must have looked pole-axed to the man. Jenny was married? Priest, what did you do? "What happened to her, if you don't mind my asking, Mister...?"

"Dave Sawyer. And I do mind, mister. It's none of your damned business. I'll get your food dished up."

He gave the cook a close look. "My apologies. Didn't mean to offend or intrude on your grief. I was just curious. She was nice when she didn't have to be and did me a kindness."

The man didn't move away from the table and that was surprising. The mourning period for his wife must not have lasted long.

He took out his new leather badge holder and laid it on the table. "My name is Coble Bray, and I'd appreciate any information you can give me."

Dave gazed at the badge a moment and then looked up. Indecision covered his face and Coble had the thought this man should never play poker. The cook acted like he wanted to leave but seemed to have trouble moving his feet. It took him a moment before he spoke.

"She died in Kansas City. Two, three times a month, she'd go there for supplies. Said she liked to ride the cars." He shrugged. "I let her go. Seemed harmless enough."

Coble put the badge holder in his shirt pocket. It was ironic. The man's late wife had told him not to go flashing it around. Now, he was doing it again. He let her go to Kansas City? From their short acquaintance, he couldn't imagine Jenny letting anyone order her around. He wondered if she had a temper like Maria's.

"Know how she died?"

The man turned fidgety and Coble didn't like it. The more he watched, the less he liked anything about a man whose gaze never landed anywhere.

"No. They shipped her down to Mindenmines on a rail car. I brought her home for the burying. There was a note on the casket saying it was an unexplained death. Just one of those things. They were sorry for my loss."

They? "Who wrote the note?"

He stood lost in thought a moment and then turned his skeptical glance on Coble. "I don't know. No one signed it. Why is that important to you?"

"You didn't wonder how she died? What happened? Any of that?"

The floor was of sudden interest to the man and Coble resisted the urge to help him look. "Seemed a little late for that by the time I knew of it. She was already gone." He looked up. "Again, why?"

For some reason, he didn't trust Dave, or his

lack of anger. He couldn't put the woman—who'd befriended him and won Priest's heart—married to this man. On the other side of the coin—stranger things have happened. A jealous husband can do uncommon things. Anger does not always come out hot.

"I'm looking into it. Curiosity is the bane of lawmen everywhere. You didn't happen to save that note, did you?"

With an exasperated look, the cook shook his head and returned to the kitchen.

Coffee came first, and a lot of it. He sat sipping while pondering the situation. He didn't know where to start. Truth is, Maria usually asked all the good questions. For his part, he was lucky enough to recognize a skunk when he saw it. He thought he smelled one now, but it was a slight odor that he couldn't pin down.

The biggest thing about this? The killer asked for him. Personal. He couldn't get his mind off that. Why? Revenge? Men had died by his hand and they had friends. That could be the key. Maybe the killer would find him soon enough. Although, he felt a stand-up fight would not happen. Now that he was here, was he caught in a web and didn't know it? Yet, he had no choice but to risk it.

The man brought his meal, refilled the mug of coffee, and left him alone. It wasn't a couple of minutes before he came back. He stood, shifting his weight foot-to-foot until Coble acknowledged him.

"Is there something else, Mr. Sawyer?"

There was a hint of sarcasm in the man's answer. "You said you were curious. Well, there's been a death that was unexplained out with the German farmers west of here. They don't talk about it. You being so curious and all, I thought you'd want to know."

He snorted. "Good luck getting any information from those square heads. They don't have much to do with us town folk."

Like he'd told Priest, there was always something more. Always another rabbit hole to explore. He shook his head. There wasn't much about his job that lifted the spirits, and yet he'd taken it again—eyes wide open.

"Can you point me to a good place for a room? I'll likely be here a while."

———

COBLE WALKED a few doors down from Jenny's Café and found a boarded-up sheriff's office. He distinctly remembered it being the building where a baby-faced killer murdered three men. It seemed an easy solution for a place to stay. Whoever did the job used short nails and the boards came away easy. The ghosts could either go out the back way or put up with another lost soul.

Stepping inside, he saw a dust-covered desk and chair and a pot-bellied stove in the middle of the floor. A bunk was situated against a wall. A door hanging on one hinge opened to the back, showing a single jail cell. It was curious to see they made the bars of saplings trimmed smooth and polished, and the door of solid wood. A strong enough contrivance, unless someone had a pocket knife and a lot of time, or pet termites.

He decided to use the office until someone kicked him out. No telling who owned the building. If anyone objected, he'd find out soon enough. He stripped his bedroll and possibles bag from the paint and tossed them inside the door. Across the street was a stable, so he led the horse through its double doors.

A tired voice greeted him from the dark interior. "Howdy."

The hostler was a man who'd ridden his last trail. Friendly blue eyes stared from a sun-bronzed, wrinkled face. He walked with a limp, reaching gnarled hands for the reins. The thumb was missing from his left hand. Coble guessed a cow-critter snapped a rope tight before the man could finish his dally around the saddle horn. Not a strange occurrence. It happened often enough in cattle country.

"Can you take care of the paint for me? He's a mite upset that I left him out in the rain."

That got a chuckle from the hostler. "Sure thing, mister. I'll bed him down, feed and water...maybe a rubdown. Looks like a good horse."

Coble grinned, shaking his head. "He is, but don't spoil him. We'll never get him to come outside again. How much?"

The man rubbed his head, moving his faded gray hat back and forth. "How's a dollar a day sound?"

"Sounds like too damned much. Look, I don't know how long I'll be here. It might be a while. At those prices, I'll pay you more than I can make in a month."

The hostler didn't seem affronted. "What's your business, if you don't mind my asking?"

The badge seemed to surprise him. Coble pointed across the muddy street. "Do you know who owns the building the sheriff's office is in?"

"Johnny Bascome did." The man stared at him a long moment. "He was the last town marshal. Of course, he just had squatters' rights. I doubt there's any paper on the place."

So, another mystery. "Was? Where is he?"

"Well, Johnny was trying to keep some law and order around these parts. Seemed dedicated about it. Good man. Honest folks liked him. Then some fellers from the new part of town formed a grievance committee and came by to see him one night. They asked him to leave town."

Coble had visions of a turtle race being faster than getting information from this man. "What happened?"

The man grinned. "Johnny left."

"Just like that? Seems a bit odd."

The hostler smiled and gazed out at the street. "You might say they were real persuasive."

It was an occurrence that played out in fast

towns. If a marshal couldn't deal with it, he might as well pack it up and leave.

"Alright, old-timer..."

"Fred Curry."

"Okay. Fred. I'm going to stay in that office while I'm in town. It'll save me money as I'm trying to figure out how to pay you for keeping my horse. If you'll be so kind as to keep the paint, I'd consider it a favor. We can settle up later."

The hostler nodded. "I can give you a special rate and put him in the corral out back—feed and water with the rest of the general stock." His smile grew. "I'm thinking a dollar a day. Lawmen don't last around here—especially marshals with fancy badges. Go a little farther south into the territory and they don't last at all."

"Well, I have a different opinion about that. I won't run away, and if I'm killed, you can always sell my horse and saddle. Would that be fair compensation?"

"Fair enough. You got a name for the headstone? I'll throw that in for the same price."

"Coble Bray."

The hostler backed away a step or two and Coble hated to see it. This was a normal, down-to-earth, good man who shouldn't be skittish at a name or reputation. A marshal should be invisible to a law-abiding citizen.

Fred's eyes were cool. "I reckon the Deacon can put his horse where he likes."

He shook his head. "Nothing like that. I'll pay a fair rate."

The hostler's smile was back and speculation came to his expression. "Maybe you will. Maybe you won't. Otherwise, that's a fine horse."

As he moved away, the man spoke again. "Deacon?"

"Price go up?"

"Nah. Just a word to the wise. You don't seem to be a bad sort. Not like some of the wannabe fast-gun artists that pass through. Anyway, there's a lot of uncommon bad men in town. And I do mean uncommon. Joplin is chasing them out and they're landing here before going on to Dodge or Abilene. The riffraff are trying to keep the law away from this town so they can run it—any way they can."

"I'll keep that in mind." Coble hesitated a moment. "I guess you knew Jenny from the café?"

"I did. Her death was a terrible thing. She was good people."

He nodded. Maybe he could stay neutral on that assumption, but in the end, it wouldn't matter. Her life was her own.

"I agree. When I met her, she treated me right. Know anyone who might want her dead?"

The hostler looked startled. "It's been told that she died in her sleep. That's the only word we had. Now, with you asking questions, I'm thinking she didn't."

He nodded, watching the man work it through his mind.

Fred took his hat off, shaking his head. "That ain't right."

The move surprised Coble. It was a little late to show respect or condolence.

The man continued. "Can't imagine anyone wanting to do her harm. Everyone liked her. You looking into that?"

He watched the man, skeptical of his reactions. "That and several things. What about her husband? He on the up and up?"

Fred's head snapped up from studying the straw-covered floor, anger clouding his eyes. "What husband? The man who's running her café was her cook. In his off hours, he tries to be a player up on the strip. Gambles a lot. They call him Slick, and it ain't a compliment."

Coble nodded, lost in thought a moment. Ideas were bouncing around his head. None of them good.

"Somehow I'm not surprised at that. So, he just took it over? No other owners?"

The hostler walked away with the horse. His voice seemed older. "None of my business."

———

COBLE GAZED EASTWARD. The way to the new part of town was open before him, but he preferred to stay away. News of his arrival preceded him, and he didn't feel like waving a red flag in front of those bulls any time soon. He could see men and horses lining the street. He'd given no thought to being a town tamer—didn't consider it his job. That was up to the locals. He was after different fish.

After strolling up and down the short street of the old part of town, he returned to the office. Sitting in the chair behind the desk, he rummaged through the drawers and then sat drumming his fingers on the top. It'd been a good desk once but now the drawers stuck. He put wax on his list of things to buy. When he checked the lamps, they were all dry, so oil went on the list too.

Sitting there was like waiting for lightning to strike. It was quiet, too quiet for the time and place. He opened the shutters on a rear window to allow air to move through the building. A piano played in the distance. He couldn't imagine how loud it would be standing next to it.

A piece of a broom propped in a corner allowed him to raise a fair amount of dust, although the broom had a twist to it from sitting on the bristles. Anyone outside might have thought there was a fire from the amount of dust that left through the windows. He vowed to take the thin mattress from the wooden-lathed bunk and beat the dust out of it, along with any critters he'd missed.

It was middle afternoon, so he headed outside to find a place to buy supplies and walked right into trouble.

A large, burly man wearing a bowler hat stood by the door, hand poised to knock. How the man could wear a checkered-wool shirt over dirty underwear in the August heat was a mystery he didn't want to explore. Two others flanked the man and wore tied-down holsters with cut-away fronts. Their hands rested on their pistols. Coble guessed they were the enforcement arm of this little welcoming committee. Neither looked like they'd done a day's worth of honest work in their lives. He took a quick glance around and saw no one else in the street.

"Congratulations, gentlemen. You got here fast."

The big man stepped back, looking confused. His voice was high-pitched and sounded strange from a man his size. Mutton chop whiskers framed a fat face set off by small, mean-looking eyes. Garters held up his long sleeves.

"You that new marshal?"

"I don't know if I'm the particular one you need. But I am a marshal." He decided this man hadn't acquitted himself well in the schoolhouse.

The large man turned slightly and grinned at his friends.

This was an old dance and he'd learned all the steps. He had time to set himself, and when the man turned back from grinning at his friends, Coble hit him. The man's shoulders hit the boardwalk first before he rolled into the street. He stood rubbing his knuckles while watching the other two men.

"If you're the welcoming committee for new visitors to your town, I'll apologize. Otherwise, you need to go back to your rat hole."

The two gunmen were staring at the man on the ground, and Coble tried again. "Look, if you can't speak, we're going to have a hard time deciding what you want. Since I don't see any fried chicken, a key to the city, or other presents from the local chamber of commerce, I'm going to assume you're trying to run me off like you did Johnny Bascome."

He held out his hand to the man struggling to rise. Setting that broken nose was going to take some work, if there was a sawbones available.

"All right. Up you go."

Maybe he could blame it on the heat. Two mistakes were made, and he should've known better. He reached to help the man up with his gun hand. The man didn't take it, slapping the offered hand away. One of the men behind him saw his chance and drew his gun.

Coble stepped to the left and palmed his pistol. The gunman's shot struck muttonchops in the back as he tried to rise. His return shot punched a hole in the shooter's left shirt pocket. The last gunman had to have set a record for the time it took him to raise his hands, and he looked ill.

Before Coble could speak, a gun fired from across the street and a man fell from between the buildings, his rifle going off into the dust. Fred stood with a Winchester pointing at the fallen man. Their gaze met across the distance.

Coble's voice sounded muffled after the noise of gunfire. "Thanks, friend."

Smoke trailed from the barrel of Fred's rifle. "I ain't your friend. Just don't like to see anyone back shot."

He disappeared into the gloom of his barn, and Coble faced the last man. Looked like his arms were getting tired.

"Put your hands down." He watched the young man a moment to see if he was going to be sick. For a moment, he thought the boy would lose that battle.

"Didn't go like you thought, did it?"

It was a moment and a couple of deep breaths before he got an answer. "No, sir. It did not."

"That's all right. It never does. Now, you need to gather up all the guns from the dead men and put them in the office."

"What about mine?"

Coble shrugged. "Do what you want. I don't think you're a back-shooter."

The would-be gunman finished his chore and then stood in the street looking lost. He was young and looked like he was about to lose his lunch again. Fred's bullet had taken his man in the throat. That was not pretty.

"What's your name?"

The young man's voice was sullen, and he didn't look up. "Fallon."

He understood the embarrassment. All those hours practicing, trying to act like a bad man, while knowing deep down it was a mistake. And he almost died for it.

"That a first name or last?"

The man shuffled his feet and stared at the ground between them. "Tom. Tom Fallon."

Coble almost smiled. He would have if the lesson hadn't been so painful for the boy. "You got horses, Tom?"

The boy nodded, alert for something to do that wouldn't get him shot.

"Well, you'd better go get them. Better yet, get their horses and a wagon. Load these men and take them back up the street to whoever hired you. Bring the extra horses and rigs back to Fred's stable. Once you do that, I'd suggest you leave town."

Tom's head jerked up at that and he stared hard at Coble, trying to get his toughness back.

He shook his head. "Look, your pride is misplaced. You're doing dirty work for someone else —someone pulling strings like you're some damned puppet. I'm letting you go. But if I see you after today, I'm going to figure you're trying to even the score."

Tom tried to stare him down. That failing, he turned and marched toward the new part of town, gaining speed as he went.

The boy was too young to know you can't measure toughness by a mean look or boastful words. Coble's gut told him that he'd be seeing the boy again. It'd be a shame. He might be a good kid, and his first instinct wasn't to pull iron along with his friend. In his mind, he probably wanted to give Coble an even break. There would be consequences for his choices in the future that would decide if he lived or died. Or became a man.

His gaze went from the shadowed opening of

the barn across the street and then to the dead man who'd tried to ambush him. Now he had a debt, whether Fred liked it or not.

He heard a noise and looked to his left. Dave was standing in front of the café. When he saw Coble watching, he stepped back inside. That situation wasn't his business today, but he had a real itch to make it so. After all, he had a shiny new badge.

Chapter Five

SUNLIGHT STREAMING THROUGH THE WINDOW OF the jail woke Coble from a night of tossing and turning on a lumpy, thin mattress. He sat up and looked at the stove. He'd completed his shopping list, but it was too hot to fire up the stove for coffee. Boiled water was the only thing he'd drink for a long time. Hopefully, the café felt the same. He'd seen the dead birds in the water trough under the windmill.

Stepping out the back door, he spied an outhouse close by. Built better than the surrounding buildings, it had milled planks held together with leather straps and hinges. It was stuck, so he had to jerk it open and then slam it back. The weeds needed watering anyway, and the smell he'd just released chased him back inside. If he stayed here very long, that outhouse had to go. It would make a nice fire if he could catch a high wind going away from the buildings.

A few men were going into the café as he strolled up. Most were cattlemen or storekeepers. A couple looked like gamblers wearing broadcloth and fancy shirts—the shirts were dirty with frayed cuffs. He couldn't guess if they were ending their night shift or starting fresh this morning. One thing he knew. Work and play never stopped in this town.

Coble decided to wait his turn at the café. He figured to keep checking in there since the eatery was the only place he and Priest both knew in Hard Times. It was still the most likely place to meet. He was worried about Priest. His friend should be here by now, and that made him irritable. The man had a half-day head start and should have arrived first. Still, no telling the things a man can run into that delay a trip. Maybe he escorted Judge MacGregor back to Kansas City, or at least to the rail line.

An older, nondescript woman in a faded dress came up to him. She had on a bright flowered apron that drew attention from everything else. Considering the apron worn by Dave Sawyer the night before, hers was a welcome sight. He didn't know what kind of flower she'd embroidered on the linen, but it was cheerful.

"You'll have to wait a bit for breakfast, if you don't mind."

He smiled at her, noticing the dark circles under her eyes and the dull brown hair with a lace-edged cloth tied on top. Her return smile was more of a grimace as she shifted from foot to foot. He wondered how many miles she'd walked this morning.

"That's alright with me, ma'am. Would you send Mr. Sawyer out to see me?"

She stepped back a pace, casting a wary glance at him. "Do you know Dave? He's awfully busy right now."

"I appreciate your loyalty. Do you know him well?" Maybe he could learn as much from her as with Dave. Her face started to blush, the red starting from her neck and working up.

"We're acquainted."

He leaned toward her. "Does he do the cooking?"

Her hands twisted a dish towel she fished out of her pocket as she shook her head. "Not usually... maybe some in the afternoons. He can't keep up in the mornings."

He showed her his badge, thinking it was a habit he wanted to break. "Then it sounds like you're doing all the work and he's standing around. Send him out. Please."

Her eyes narrowed before she turned, and her heels banged away on the plank floor. A softer shoe would help her feet. Surely she knew that.

Dave peeked around the door frame to the kitchen and then slowly edged out. Coble took him by the arm and propelled him outside. The man dug in his heels and struggled a moment.

"Don't do that, Mr. Sawyer. We're going to have a little talk."

He looked around, making sure they had some privacy. The rising sun was an orange ball resting on top of the street when he looked east toward the new part of town. He turned back to Dave, blinking his eyes. Why he gazed at that blazing light, he didn't know, except to reassure himself it was going to be a blistering day.

"You lied to me. I want to know why."

The whiny voice didn't give the morning a good start. "That ain't none of your...."

He slammed Dave against the wall. Something clattered on the floor inside the building. "Try again."

A couple of men came out the door and gave them a curious look. Seemed no one liked Dave enough to intervene.

The man shrugged, trying to straighten his shirt and side-step Coble's hand. "Some folks don't like that I took over the café. That's all. Hell, it was just sitting here with nobody to run it."

"Maybe because they think you had something to do with Jenny's death?"

His eyes slid away a moment. A lie was coming. "I didn't. That's the truth."

"Is there another kind?" Coble watched him a moment. Her death might be a convenient way to get ownership of a cash cow to feed his gambling habit. And people didn't generally tell you they were honest unless they weren't. Maybe not a direct involvement, but something didn't match up.

"Alright. I'll let that go for now, but don't ever lie

to me, Dave. I don't like it. The next thing is this. There's a friend of mine coming to town. He'll be asking you questions about Jenny. He's less tolerant of lies than me. But don't worry. He'll give you absolution for whatever you've done."

"What are you accusing me of? I ain't done nothing wrong."

He nodded. "Maybe. But understand this. Jenny didn't die natural, and I'm betting she had a lot of friends. We're going to find her killer. If you know something...anything, you'd better be telling it. If I catch you lying again, I'm going to squeeze you until there's nothing left inside. That's a promise."

Dave had a pensive look on his face when he went back inside. Coble didn't blame him. The man was guilty about something. He'd let Priest sort it out. He owed him that.

The night before, he'd wondered if the café had enough business to survive. He needn't have worried. A solid procession of customers were going in and out of the café. There was good food here. You'd think people would take more time to savor it.

The wait for a table lasted a few minutes, and then he had to share it with a man better suited for a trough, who ended up with more food on his whiskers than in his gullet. Maybe he was saving it for later?

His eating companion wore rough lace-up boots like he'd seen men wear working on timber and clothes unwashed since they were new—a long time ago. There couldn't be that many trees around here, and he was curious. It looked as if he labored at something, and Coble was sure it was honest labor.

"Do you work around here, friend?"

The man just paused in chewing a moment, stared at him, and didn't answer. The bright side was it only took him about three minutes to eat. Coble enjoyed his meal alone, if he could purge the sight and smell of his eating partner from his mind. The café was clearing out. Seems daylight was late to breakfast.

Tired of waiting for Priest to show up, he left and stood on the boardwalk in front of the café. He thought of leaving instructions with Dave but felt the man would never pass them on. The stable across the street was busy with riders leading their horses out to pound away toward the north. He knew cattle ranches were out that way. As he stood leaning on a post, more riders came in and left their horses with Fred Curry and then walked briskly up the street to the new town. He'd heard the gambling houses were open all night and day, he wondered if the whores worked in shifts...or just worked until they dropped—or died.

He thought of walking up to the saloons and knew he'd have to make an appearance sometime, but he put it off. His welcome in the new town would be dicey at best. Still, he had more important things to take care of. A murder in the German settlement. A strange murder.

Waiting until the rush at the stable had calmed

down, he walked over to see Fred and wake up his horse. If the paint wasn't moving, it was sleeping. Maybe it held the same dim view of the world as he and didn't want to watch it.

The sun tried its damnedest to bake the offending moisture from the soil, and the swirling air was hot as a Cheyenne spirit lodge, but it was still a beautiful morning. He filled his lungs with fresh, humid air, glad to be alive. In the time it took to expel the breath, thoughts of Maria dampened his mood. He couldn't think of a good answer to that problem. That he loved her was a given, but there were things they'd never agree on.

Maybe he'd made a mistake in letting her push him into marriage. That burden of thought wouldn't leave his shoulders anytime soon. Was there a set of rules for this game? After she threw him out, should he have waited in the hills to go back later, full of contrition and apology? Did she give him a meal thinking he'd be home for breakfast? If he were a love-sick boy that might be the case. Frail though it was, his pride wouldn't let him do that. Forgiveness was a given, but you never forget the cause.

Thoughts of a mouse navigating a maze came to him. He didn't know what was at the end of the labyrinth—a reward or trap.

One decision came easy. Her temper might subside after a few days of his absence. He vowed to go home if quick answers weren't forthcoming in Hard Times. He never liked mysteries anyway. The judge be damned.

———

OXFORD GRAHAM SAT in an over-sized chair behind the ornate, polished cherry wood desk of Judge MacGregor. He'd been shuffling through papers for an hour, finally dropping papers on the slick surface of the desk to see how far they would slide. If the judge didn't show up soon, he'd have to start playing with the secretary to relieve the boredom.

On cue, voices came from the outer office.

"Judge, there's a man waiting for you."

A low, rumbling voice replied. "Alice, you know not to let anyone in there."

"He didn't ask, sir. Just walked in. But he seems nice enough."

Judge MacGregor moved into the room, ducking under the doorway and stopping in front of the desk. His unbuttoned black revealed a plaid shirt beneath.

"Get out from behind my desk."

Oxford smiled and pointed toward the door. "Close it. We have some business to discuss."

"Business? I don't know you, so I can't imagine what it would be."

"All of which you'll find out when you close the door."

The judge stared a moment and then turned to close the door.

"Good. Now we can talk." Oxford moved some papers around. "I've looked through all your little cubbyholes and can't find anything about annulments. I must say your filing system leaves something to be desired."

The judge moved around the side of the desk, eyeing the intruder. "Not much call for that. Can't remember doing one, so I'd just write it out. Now, if you'd get up, perhaps I could find something."

As the big man moved toward him, Oxford almost laughed. He couldn't be more obvious. The giant probably thought himself impervious to physical harm because of his size and saw himself throwing the intruder out of the door. As the judge reached for him, Oxford stood and pulled out a leather sap, striking the judge where his neck joined his shoulder. The judge dropped to his knees with a gasp, shoulder slumping.

"Well, from the expression on your face, I'd say that is painful. And that's just your first broken bone of the day. Don't try it again."

He helped the dazed man into his chair. He had to keep him off balance. A simple shout to his secretary could ruin his plans.

"Now, your right hand is still serviceable. Write it out nice and pretty with all the right words. An annulment of marriage."

The judge fumbled for paper and ink. "This is useless. You must know it won't stand in a court of law."

He tapped the man on his head with the sap. "Not your problem. Just write it up. Here, I'll help steady the paper. It's hard to do one-handed."

"I must protest—"

The tap to the head came harder. He'd have to be careful to not kill the man. "Your lack of attention is bothersome."

The judge shook his head a moment. "Alright. Who are the parties involved?"

Oxford smiled. "Coble Bray and Maria Santos."

The judge gasped. "Why? Who are you? They should be here to present this themselves. You cannot do this."

He hit the man on his injured shoulder, bringing another gasp. "Here you are worrying about things of no concern. Write it."

A few minutes later, the judge had the paper in hand and called out, "Alice. Please come in."

She walked through the door, staring at the judge and tall man standing beside him. "Yes?"

He sighed and slumped in his chair. "I need you to witness this document."

"Is everything alright, Judge? You don't look good." She stood hesitant at the door.

Oxford smiled at her. "We are discussing some distressing news, Alice. Don't be concerned."

Taking the paper, she looked it over with raised eyebrows and then signed at the bottom. Casting another curious glance at them, she closed the door as she left.

The judge looked up at him. "You've got your damned paper. Now get out."

"Not yet. I'm curious. I looked through your papers and news clippings while waiting. There's quite a lot of it. I found so much murder and mayhem, it's depressing. And the murder of inno-cents in such gruesome and novel ways?" You've made quite a study of them. I don't know how you cope with all that."

"I asked your name." The judge's hand inched toward a desk drawer.

"Now you're afraid? Now you're trying to resist?" Oxford shook his head, smiling for a moment, and then pointed across the room. "I found your pistol and set it on the counter. It's unloaded of course. We wouldn't want any accidents to happen."

"And my name doesn't matter. It isn't in any of those articles. Should be, but it's not. Those are just the names of people that were stupid enough to get caught."

The judge stared at him, wide-eyed, breath coming in short gasps, and then he tried to come out of his chair. Oxford settled him down with another tap to his head.

He lay a small cross on the table. "It's time, Judge. We need to end this part of the game."

The judge's eyes widened, staring at the cross. "What do you mean? What's that for?"

Oxford's chuckle was nearly a giggle of excite-ment. "I know you've seen a cross like that when you and that minister went to see Coble. You know what it is. It was a shame about Jenny, but I needed a messenger. She wasn't pretty like your Alice, but she was very energetic."

He leaned toward the judge, his voice soft and

gentle. "I need you to put the cross in your mouth. I've heard it's quite painless and over quickly."

"No." The judge shook his head, struggling to lift his arms. "I will not."

Nodding, he chuckled and then smiled. "Of course you will. It's your only choice. You have a wife. Oh, I know you don't care much for her. Your dalliances with your secretary and a few others are well known. I could use your wife or even kill her, but it wouldn't mean anything to you. Just a small disturbance in your life."

Oxford chuckled. "I have to admire the setup here. Your offices are very private, and that Alice looks to be a spicy little thing. I'd wager you've had a lot of fun with her. Quite a size difference—like you're using a child. Is that what you like, Judge?"

"But I bet you'd sacrifice her in a moment, if it came to it." He tapped the judge harder on the head with the sap and then held it up before his eyes. "This little contrivance kills and hardly leaves a mark and, as you know, is quite painful. Just look at a giant like you. You can hardly use your arms. You are helpless."

The judge stared at him with tears coursing down his cheeks. His left collar bone was broken and his arm hung loose, palm up.

Oxford's gaze hardened. "You have children."

The judge's panicked eyes searched the killer's face. "Why? What in God's name...?"

"Oh, it's not complicated." He waved the annulment paper. "This is just another piece of a puzzle, and you—well, you're a loose end."

Another tap on the head shook the judge. "Come on now. This is the fun part. You get to save your children and give your wife her freedom from a philandering husband. She'll be ecstatic, after a proper mourning period of course. Do the right thing. Isn't that what you're all about? Doing the right thing?"

The only sound in the room was the judge's labored breathing. It took a few moments before his hand moved toward the cross with the brown tip on it...and stopped.

His voice was hoarse. "Why the cross? The poison. Why not just kill me? The way my head hurts, I don't have long to live anyway."

"I guess it won't matter if I tell you, but...I won't. It's a remembrance. Quite the game piece, don't you think?"

He moved the cross closer to the judge. "Come now. All waiting is at an end and I have things to do. Put it in your mouth, or I'll crush your skull and then put it in. The results will be the same. I think it's quite painless. Not that I've tried it."

Oxford lied. It did appear painful—for just a moment.

He cleared off some space on the desk before stepping to the door. "Alice, could you come in please? Seems the judge is ill."

———

MARIA STEPPED into the town marshal's office in Kansas City. The room was large, with several desks and a long counter separating the workers from the public. A gray-haired woman standing behind the counter raised her eyebrows in question.

"Something we can do for you?"

She wondered if this woman's lot in life was better than her own. From her gray bun and faded blue dress buttoned tight to her throat, down to scuffed shoes peeking from beneath her hem, she looked dull. Maybe dealing with the public every day would do that. For her peace of mind, Maria hoped she was safe from the predators of the world.

Maria smiled, nodding. "I'm looking for Tom Speers."

The woman looked at her a moment and then turned her head and yelled. "Tom."

A small man came bouncing out of an office, spied her, and held out his hand. "Tom Speers. How can I help you?"

He was looking her over and she wondered how he classified her. She dressed simply, much like the lady behind the counter, except brighter—more alive. Tom Speers must have liked what he saw because he tried to stand taller, resembling a Bantam rooster preening for his hens. The gray-lady beside him snorted and walked away. Maria liked her now.

She shook his hand, having trouble extricating from his grip. "I'm Maria Bray."

That brought his gaze up to hers. "Bray? An uncommon name."

She nodded. "Coble's wife."

He deflated to just plain rooster with worry lining his face. "Is he around? I could use him about now. We've had a couple of strange murders."

It was hard to keep the anger from her voice. "No. He's not with me. He's off investigating some other strange murders. There doesn't seem to be any lack of them."

The man just grunted. "True. What can I do for you?"

"I'm looking for Priest. He's a friend of ours and I don't know where he lives. I wondered if you knew where to find him?"

At the marshal's blank look, she tried again. "Pastor August Schuler. Used to have a church in the city? After it closed, he moved, and I don't know where."

His expression went from blank to guarded. "Why do you want to know?"

"What difference does it make? He's a friend of mine and Coble's. I'd like to talk to him. This is not a complicated request. Has something happened?"

The marshal's gaze traveled around the office, finally returning to her. "Mr. Schuler was shot early this morning while saddling his horse. It appeared he was leaving for a trip. We've got him locked away for now because we don't know who did it, or why."

She clutched the counter to keep from falling.

Priest shot? He was supposed to have Coble's back. Now, he'd be alone, and she should be with him.

"Take me to Priest. Please. It's very important."

He regarded her a moment before turning and grabbing a deputy by the arm. "Take Mrs. Bray to the infirmary to see Mr. Schuler. Make sure no one follows."

The deputy needed lessons in checking his back trail, but she did not. Nothing looked suspicious, and a few minutes later, she stood by Priest's bedside, watching a nurse wipe sweat from his forehead. He looked pale and lifeless. Maria took a big breath and then regretted it. The air in the room reeked of soiled bedclothes, alcohol, and infection. She repressed an urge to go open a window.

"Has he been awake?"

The woman glanced at her for a moment. "Not since this morning. The doctor is keeping him sedated so he won't move and break open the wound. Maybe tomorrow or the next day would be better to visit."

"I don't have that much time. How bad is it? Will he live?"

The nurse stood and tapped a place on her side, just above the hip. "The bullet took him here. He'll be alright if we can keep the infection down, but he lost a lot of blood. It will take a while for him to recover."

"The marshal said they didn't know who did it. Did he say anything to you—any ideas?"

The nurse shook her head and sat down. "No

idea. There are many bad men in this city. Why they'd shoot a padre, I do not know."

The woman looked worried, constantly smoothing wrinkles in the bedclothes, wiping his brow, keeping busy. "He killed a man a few days ago in a bar fight. Maybe it is retaliation? Who knows?"

She turned her gaze to Maria. "I am having trouble matching the man I used to know with what I see. I used to hear him preach. Now..."

"Well, good luck with that." Maria paused a moment. "And open a window. He likes fresh air."

She stood in front of the infirmary, wondering where to go next. Would Oxford contact her here? Or should she travel to Hard Times. She gave a startled yelp when a man took her elbow and started walking.

"Is your friend still alive?"

She gasped and pulled free, confronting the man. Nothing had changed. Still tall with a bland, innocent face and mischievous eyes. Topped by a low-crowned, gray hat. She knew his surprised expression was fake and everything he did was for show.

"Oxford? How did you find me so soon?"

He spread his hands with a smile. "You can catch anything with the proper bait. I knew you'd check in with your friend when you arrived, once you knew of his injuries. So here I am."

"It was a courtesy call, no more." The proper bait? She stopped, searching his eyes. "Did you shoot Priest?"

He laughed. "You know I wouldn't do that. At least not directly. The man has enemies. They just needed a little motivation and it was the best way to put you in a place I could find you. This is a pretty big city."

It was hard to catch her breath and she needed to get control of herself. A woman killed and a taunt sent to Coble. Now Priest was out of commission. And a man she knew as a deadly killer was posing in front of her and having fun. She'd seen him work before at keeping people off balance and confused, like a carnival shell game—watching the pea.

"I assumed you wanted me to see the key. What do you want of me? Why are you here? We were through a long time ago."

Oxford smiled. "You would not believe how delighted I was to find you as one of the players in this drama. And to answer your question, I'm just moving my game pieces around to where they can be the most helpful. As for us? I thought we'd take a little trip together. We'll have a nice train ride down to Joplin, then a quick buggy ride over to Hard Times to finish our business."

She stood a moment, searching his eyes. "You've been to this town? Hard Times?"

"A delightful little place. You'll love it."

If he'd already been there, it was a trap, and Coble was walking right into it. She had to get a message to him. "Why should I go anywhere with you?"

His eyes lost their mirth. "Because you'll be dead if you don't. It would be foolish to cross me."

They stopped at a small restaurant with outside tables. "First, you need to see this."

She took the paper offered to her, amazed her hand wasn't shaking. Glancing from it to the man's face, she flushed under his scrutiny.

"Annulment? That's impossible. Why on earth...?"

He gave her a satisfied smirk. "Signed by Judge MacGregor himself. And witnessed by his assistant. You remember the judge? Giant of a man? He was the root that started all your troubles. And too nosy for his own good. So, yes. It's very possible. Hardly any trouble at all."

Her mind whirled, trying to figure things out, but it was like trying to wade through quicksand. This was a mistake unless she could turn it to her advantage. Why not stay close? He'd most likely kill her anyway. If she played along, maybe she could reverse the tables. This man liked games? She'd play one. Now she had to think of Coble. That was her end game.

"Why am I part of this? Why do you need the marriage annulled?"

He gave a gentle laugh. "The main reason is to make him angry. But it's not really a game—more like gamesmanship. And once all the pieces are in place, the game will be over. Not being able to solve a simple murder will disgrace him. People won't trust him and will shun him. And then, to make it worse, I'll have his woman and rub his nose in it."

"He's smarter than that." Her heart pounded in her chest. "And I'll never be yours. Not like that."

He patted her hand. "Of course you will. But it's not just you, although you're icing on the cake."

Pausing, he continued. "There are other things."

"I can't believe this. Did you kill Jenny? Priest's woman?"

He nodded once, shrugged. "It was necessary. I needed to deliver a message. It was unfortunate. She was nice." His smile got bigger. "Once it happened, I knew the Priest would go to his Deacon."

She wondered how quick she could get away. If she turned him in, would it make any difference? There was no proof. Once they found out her past with him, she'd be labeled as someone lying to get revenge.

His hand was still on her icy fingers as she threw out her weak reply. "I'll go to Marshal Speers and the judge. You'll be arrested, and we'll have this reversed."

"I'm sorry. The Honorable Judge MacGregor met with an untimely accident. It was a death in chambers. His last act was to sign your release."

She gasped. Another killing. "Let me go. I don't want a release from my marriage. All I want is a normal life...away from you."

Breath was hard to come by as she felt tears running down her cheeks. Why didn't she tell Coble about this man? Why didn't she just run...? Why didn't—

"Don't try to outthink me, Maria. You never could. But it is fun when you try."

"I can go to the marshal. He'll help me."

"Help you with what? There's no proof that I've been anything but a concerned friend. What on earth could you tell him?"

He clapped his hands. "So, let's go pick up your valise and take care of your horse. Then we can be on our way. And while we're at it, why don't you give me your pistol? It won't weigh down your pocket so much. It makes your dress hang funny, and you're much too beautiful for that. Oh, and the derringer from your clutch."

She took a deep, shuddering breath. Her priority was to find a way to get a message to Coble and warn him. Outthink Oxford? No. But she could be there at the end or, given a chance, kill him. She wouldn't lose anything but her pride...or maybe her life.

Chapter Six

COBLE HAD HEARD GERMANS LIKED THINGS KEPT neat and precise. He had no experience with that until he saw the farms. The best word he could think of was tidy. Most fields were small and fenced in, something one or two people could take care of. He wondered if they had herds of goats or sheep to keep the grass short under the fences.

He turned west on a rutted lane and saw a team of horses laboring about a half mile ahead, pulling something that looked like a stone boat with teeth on the front. Standing in his stirrups, he decided they surveyed all the plots of farmland squares, with a mile on each side. Neat and tidy.

The contraption approaching did a good job of tearing up and then smoothing out the dirt on the road. When he rode by with a wave, the man driving the team looked at the prints the paint left on the finished road and then back at Coble. His gestures did not seem friendly.

Dave's directions led him to a well-kept farm with *Neumann* printed in black paint on a white-board fence. The paint had run on the letters so it looked like the fancy writing lawmakers used. The scene made him miss his ranch and Maria. Or, at least what he imagined his home might be with proper care. His chances of going back to that idyllic circumstance seemed remote.

As he approached the house, he faltered a moment and not from nostalgia. A woman sat in a rocker on the front porch, nursing a baby. She was pretty in a sturdy way, with reddish hair and blue eyes. As he drew close, he could see freckles. A lot of freckles. Her black dress was open in the front, showing a white undergarment, one side pulled down for the baby. The baby was naked except for a diaper and had a mop of dark hair. She made no attempt to cover up, and he didn't pretend to look elsewhere. As a practical matter, he figured that black dress was plenty hot on a day like this and didn't begrudge her a little ventilation.

He tipped his hat to her. "Are you Mrs. Neumann?"

"I'm Mary Neumann." She paused a moment, watching him as she pulled a cloth over her chest and baby. "It would be polite if you'd stop staring."

Bad moods are hard to overcome, and he'd started the morning with one. "Yes, ma'am. I suppose it would. What would be more convenient for me to watch? Perhaps these daisies growing along the porch? They're less beautiful than you, and I doubt they'll respond to my questions."

She rose from her chair, leaving it rocking behind her. The baby never paused in its single-minded purpose.

"Who are you, mister? What do you want?"

"My name is Coble Bray. I'm a marshal." He showed her his fancy badge. "The better question would be, why am I here?"

She didn't seem impressed with his polished trinket. He took a perverse pleasure in that. He wasn't either.

"Are you one of Judge Parker's men?"

He shouldn't have been surprised. Everyone knew of the Hanging Judge and his minions—an army of deputies dying at a staggering rate.

"No, ma'am. I am not."

Looking at him a moment and then toward one of the other farms, she nodded as she seemed to come to a decision. "I'm not supposed to talk to anyone without an Elder present. They say it's not proper. To hell with them and their ways. Come inside. I'll put the baby down and we can talk. I suppose this is about Hans?"

He thought about the Elder comment, wishing Priest were here to help navigate. He'd have some insight into that. "Hans was your husband?"

"Who else?"

Her mood seemed to be worse than his, so he kept his voice neutral. He figured she'd been through enough. "Then, yes. I'd like a few words."

He stepped down from the paint, tied him to the hitch rail, and followed her inside. It was a well-put-together house. So was she—and she didn't put much effort into hiding it. The boards on the porch were solid, and the metal hinges on the door didn't screech when she opened it. It took a good blacksmith to make those.

Her late husband was someone who had a better-than-average feel for carpentry. He paused a moment to feel the door jamb, smoothly planed and soaked with oil. The smell of fresh bread and cinnamon wafted over him as they moved inside. His stomach growled, though he'd just eaten breakfast. She turned and gave him a tentative smile.

After pointing at the kitchen table, she brought a couple mugs of coffee and a slice of warm bread with a dab of butter melting on top. As he reached for the bread, she was pushing sugar and a small pot of cream toward him.

He shook his head. "Thanks, but I take my coffee black." The bread and butter melted in his mouth and, for a moment, overwhelmed his senses. With her obvious talents, this woman wouldn't stay a widow long.

She tried to be calm but couldn't carry the act. Her folded hands rested on the table in front of her, fingers white with strain. He was glad she'd buttoned her dress. An intelligent conversation would be impossible if she hadn't. Her fingers went to her arms as she clasped her hands tight and folded her arms under her breasts. That kind of grip would leave bruises.

Married he may be, but not dead. He was surprised when she met his gaze with a direct stare, and he wondered why his life was full of conflicting women.

Her voice was soft. "What do you want to know?"

She seemed about as friendly as the man pulling that stone boat. It didn't surprise him. People were clannish. It was natural. America was supposed to be a melting pot of different peoples. At least, that's what the politicians preached. It was rare if that happened. The Irish would stay together, the same with Germans or Chinese—even different tribes of Indians. All different and staying that way.

"I'd like you to tell me the story of what happened to your husband. Anything could be helpful. Please don't leave anything out."

"Some of it is—"

"I'm sorry. I know it's hard for you."

She raised her hand at his interruption. "Not really. I was going to say some of the story is very personal. So, to continue?"

She pinned him with a steady gaze. He wasn't sure she'd blinked. Some people can do that. And snakes and lizards. He tried to not blink and failed. A lesson learned. Never try and best someone at their own game. Like wrestling pigs. You're going to get dirty.

"To be clear, my husband was an overbearing,

pompous ass." Her fingers released her arm and picked at something on her sleeve. "Wearing black is for my neighbors' benefit. Not mine. They tell me six months would be proper. Were it my choice, I'd be celebrating in bright colors and spinning a parasol on the boardwalk of some lively town."

Surprised, he looked at her a moment, running her accent through his mind. Then he smiled. "What's an Irish lass of uncertain temperament doing with a German farmer?"

She shrugged, inclining her head toward him in acknowledgment, leaning on her brogue a little harder. Far from smiling, she at least looked as if she wouldn't be shooting me.

"It was simple enough. He bought me. Or, my indenture. Same thing. Then he took a liking to me, I guess. He married me. I was surprised at that—didn't expect it. Of course, he did not ask my opinion or consent on the matter and never let me forget my place. I'm sure the marriage assured his place in the church."

Coble watched her as her expression traveled from sad to defiant. He thought of something Priest had told him once. Everyone is afraid of something. Everyone. They've lost...they've loved. He wondered if she was sure how she felt about her late husband. Finally, he shrugged.

"I don't understand. Slavery went out with the war. Hell, it was illegal and dying out anyway." He paused a moment. "Not to put too fine a point on it, but nearly as many slaves were held by the North as with the South. Many slaves never saw freedom until well after the war, especially in New York. I never understood that conflict."

Her look reduced him to primary school. "Slavery was ended for the blacks, but not the Irish. Slavery is still legal, especially for women. They call it indenture to pay off some debt, either real or imagined, but there's not much choice in the matter, and no woman's debt ever gets paid. Many are given the choice of being committed to an asylum for such things as reading a book or female vapors or going into indenture."

Long fingers twirled part of her long hair as she stared. He didn't know if she saw him or some memory she didn't care for. After a long moment, she centered her gaze on him.

"My parents needed money, so they signed a paper giving a man the authority to act in my best interest."

Her laugh was more of a grunt. "Best interest? He brought twenty of us to Kansas City. Our indentures? Sold at an auction. I'm sure he made a tidy profit. Some say we had a choice. If there was, I could never find it. We were held as prisoners until sold."

Her gaze held him. "I was lucky, I suppose. Some were bought by the bawdy houses and taken away to work until they died."

He stared at her a moment and then waved his hand for her to continue. He knew of such things but never heard a firsthand account. It was always a *Back East, Big City* thing to him.

"And your husband?"

"He died about a month ago. It was about sundown when I heard someone ride up and begin talking to Hans. He'd gone out to take his evening pipe. The tone sounded friendly enough, but I couldn't understand what they said. I was cleaning the kitchen after supper and the baby was asleep. There was a loud thump outside, like something fell against the wall, and I started toward the door."

He stopped her a moment. "No sounds of a fight? No shouting? No one was angry?"

She gave him an exasperated glance. "As I said, no. The door opened, and a man came in. He was tall and dressed in black—head to toe. His face was in shadow from his hat...I only had a single lantern burning by the stove. As he walked in, he stepped over and turned down the flame."

He wondered what kind of hat but didn't want to interrupt again. The lady had a quick temper, and he didn't want to test it.

For the first time, her eyes welled up with tears. "I didn't move...couldn't for some reason. Petrified and don't know why. When you can't see someone's eyes, you can't tell who they are or...what they are. He held his finger to his lips for me to be quiet and then pushed me toward this table. It was like looking at a snake, waiting for it to strike. I remember my chest hurt because I didn't take a breath. To this day, I don't know why I was so afraid."

He couldn't understand how someone could come in and do that. Maria would have left the man scratched and bleeding from head to toe, or he thought she would. But this woman had a baby to protect—and herself. And didn't fight. Had her servitude taught her not to fight?

"He never said a word?"

One hand went to her chest and the other to the table to steady herself. She took a calming breath. "He did...he said Hans sent him in...for me. I...I was so scared. Irish are treated bad. We're used to it. But I've never been so afraid in my life. I looked around, and there was nothing to use as a weapon. I'm ashamed to say I'm not sure I'd have used one."

She stared at her cup of coffee. Cold by now, as was his. He prompted her to finish, given the fact she was here and apparently unharmed, at least physically. Her state of mind was still in doubt.

"What happened then?"

"He used me...turned me around and bent me over this very table." She looked at him through eyes heavy with tears. "Threw my dress up over my back like a common whore, with no more feeling than shaking your hand and saying hello."

Her body shuddered, like a cold chill settled on her. "I just...submitted. To this day, I don't know why?"

Coble gave her a moment before continuing. His assessment of her rose a bit. In his experience, most women wouldn't be this strong, or living alone after the murder and her treatment.

"After it was over, did you see anything that would help us find this man?"

She shook her head, staring out the window. "When he left, it was a few moments before I went outside to check on Hans. When he didn't come in, I grew concerned. Up until then, I thought he'd sent that man inside—that they'd struck a deal. After all, I was just chattel to him."

He shook his head, glad he'd never met Hans. "Had anything like that happened before?"

"No. He'd talked of it when he was drinking and mad at me. Threatened it a few times...said he could make extra money. Anyway, when I went to check on him, he lay on the porch. Looked asleep...except he wasn't. I couldn't wake him up."

Her eyes were large on a face drained of color. "That man killed my husband and then came in and used me. Then he left. It's just so...cold."

A watery gaze searched his face. "Why didn't he kill me?"

He cleared his throat, dealing with his own conflict. His urge was to comfort...or kill. Depending on the object.

"I don't have an answer to that—wish I did. Perhaps the best answer is he didn't want to."

She hugged herself hard and shivered, her eyes haunted by the memory. He'd seen that look once on a man who'd lost his homestead, wife, and children...everything. The soul can only take so much, then it's just—gone. Her voice was a low rasp. "I was fertile."

Was fertile echoed in his mind. "How long ago did this happen again?"

"A little over a month." She put a level gaze on him. "You're wondering how I know I'm fertile? My baby is seven months old, Marshal. That a woman can't conceive while nursing is an old tale, and not a very good one. I know my body." Her eyes slid back to watching out the window. "I keep praying for the monthly. So far, God is laughing at me."

He reached out and touched her hand. "Crying maybe. Not laughing."

With a shrug, she pulled away. "When I found Hans, I started screaming until a neighbor came over."

How many times in a conversation could he wish Maria was with him? While Maria wouldn't qualify as normal, she would know how to talk to a woman —what questions to ask. He couldn't think of much else to ask. He knew Mary didn't act as he'd expect. How could she? Was there a normal for something like this? Why didn't she fight? How could she submit? His last thought made him angry at himself. He had no doubt that resisting would have meant her death. She did the best she could.

He knew it was a question having no answer. He'd heard of women killing themselves to avoid a rape, or soon after. The reasons would differ for each. His experience was that frontier women were strong and resilient and would choose how they wanted things to play out. His instinct was that Mary was stronger than she knew and would come out of this experience alright, if somewhat battered. Given a chance.

An overbearing husband can take the life right out of a woman. Sometimes it works both ways. This was hard to get his head around. Any perceived skill he owned was with guns, horses... and understanding the vagaries of men. Women always escaped his feeble attempts to figure them out.

Something about the way she avoided his eyes told him there was more. She was keeping something back. "Mary, you have my promise. Whatever you tell me will not be common knowledge. Is there something else?"

An honest person holding a lie wants to make it right. They can't stand themselves if they don't. So far, hers was a lie of omission.

"He told me to tell the other women what he did...to me. Like he was prideful of it." Her sob was more a cough. "He said to tell them not to resist if he came calling at night and he'd let their husbands live."

His immediate and simple thought was of catching him in a trap. "Has he come back?"

She shook her head. "I think he's done enough damage here."

"What about your neighbors? Know of any visits they might have had?"

Her gaze was steady. "I didn't tell them. I could

not. There have been no more killings, so who knows?"

"Was there anything else? You said your husband was on the porch and you didn't hear anything but his fall. You said there was no shot. Stabbed? Knocked out? Any idea of what happened to him?"

She stood and walked to the counter. When she came back, she held a rusted Deputy US Marshal's badge. Startled, he stared a moment. Digging into this vest pocket, he pulled out a pouch, opened it, and had her drop in the badge. When it clinked against the contents, her eyes widened.

"Collecting trinkets?"

"Yes, ma'am. In a way, I suppose I am. There have been others. Seems this killer likes to leave a remembrance." He could see her turning that information over in her mind.

"So, why are you collecting them?"

"I'm hoping it's a self-limiting endeavor." He paused to give her a level gaze. "I plan to give them back to the killer."

Another mystery. The killer changed his calling card from a cross to a key, and now a badge. The conclusion didn't take long. The cross and note were to taunt Priest, who would then come to Coble. That was easy. And the badge was to taunt Coble, maybe to prove the killer as a murderer of marshals. There was no note with the killing of the farmer Neumann, but the badge was a direct enough message. All of it was to draw attention. Crazy wouldn't begin to describe the killer.

But the cross with a key? The key was the wild card that made no sense.

———

HE SWUNG into the saddle while Mary stood on the porch. Was it bravery or madness on her part to stay in a place the killer may visit again? And if neither of those—then why? One thing he'd learned tracking men and animals. Figure out their motivation and that would tell you their next move. The Indian hunters, especially the Apache, did it all the time. He supposed it applied to women and men. What do they gain from acting a certain way?

Coble shivered at another thought. If an animal is hungry, where does it feed? What is it hungry for? This animal was hungry for death, and crowded places gave the most opportunity and offered a greater chance of getting away with it.

Another question came to him. "When the man came in the door, you said he was all in black. Is there anything else? What kind of hat did he have? High peak or low?"

She thought a moment. "Low, not a wide brim."

There are different kinds of hats, but not that many styles. Men staying in the city usually wore a smaller hat from necessity. It was next to impossible to maneuver through a crowded place with a wide-brimmed Mexican hat or some of the Stetsons. The Civil War introduced the smaller, low-crowned hat for cavalry units. Not a bowler hat, but still about as useful as telling him it was Smith, not Jones.

"So, a town hat?"

Her voice was tired and raspy. Whatever he was trying to do, she was tired of it. "I suppose."

"And his voice?"

She gave a long sigh. "Low, almost a whisper. For some reason, it was more frightening than a shout." She paused, meeting his gaze. "Much like yours."

That was an association he didn't like. "And did he hurt you in any way? Physically? I mean, other than..."

Her gaze dropped and a blush colored her face. "When I think of it...other than the violation...no. You might call him gentle but persistent."

From that comment, he knew this was a recurring nightmare for her. An occurrence she'd pick apart in her mind like a scab, turning over every thread of thought until it lay bare. With no understanding at the end.

Her attention centered over his shoulder on a rider coming across the fields and jumping a few fences to do it. They were low and split-rail, but he was good enough to be showing off some. His circuitous route finally brought him to the front of the cabin.

"You Marshal Bray?" His voice was adolescent though he looked more than twenty years old. He'd taken the time to position his wide-brimmed hat to a jaunty angle. A thin leather string kept it snug on his head.

"I am."

"There's a cottonwood grove on the east side of the new town, down by the creek. A man said to fetch you to see a body. Someone's been murdered."

Who knew he was here, and why did they care if he saw this body? If someone looked at the new town, and from what he'd heard, they'd think a body was a common occurrence.

"Who sent you?"

The young man shrugged, holding his horse in check. "Didn't know the man. He told me where to find you."

"What did he look like? Can you tell me how he was dressed?"

The young man shook his head, not speaking.

Now that was strange. Was he paid not to say? He tried again. "Young, old, tall, short, fat...?"

The boy shook his head, impatient to leave. "Didn't really notice."

He held up two fingers. "How many fingers do you see?"

The snicker and then outright laugh from the widow probably didn't help. He sighed but tried anyway. "Did the man have a name?"

"Already said I didn't know him. He didn't offer...I didn't ask."

"What's your name?"

He shook his head again—grinned again. Shrugged again. "I'm just the messenger."

He was beginning to think the boy was simple. When Coble woke this morning, he didn't remember hoping to play games but seemed to be in one. And Fred was right, his day was not getting better. He was in a strange play, unlikely in its beginning and the ending not written. And it was true what they said, plans made in the morning tend to go astray in the afternoon.

"You're not giving me much information, young man. Are you German?" When the boy didn't answer, he continued. "I'll be there when I can."

The horse danced a little, and the boy reined it under control. "You need to hurry, Marshal. The man said to hurry."

Now that was curious. Did the messenger know more than he was telling? "Why? You can't kill a man twice. If someone took the time to send for me, I expect the area will be trampled by the time I get there. So...there's no point in hurrying. I'll be there as soon as I can."

Watching the young man on the dancing horse, he couldn't stop himself. "Why don't you use the road?"

He looked at Coble like he was crazy and the world knew it. "Mister. It's Tuesday. It's grading day. You don't mess up the roads on grading day." Shaking his head, the boy took off at a gallop, back the way he came.

Shaking his head, Coble glanced at Mary.

She shrugged and nodded. "It's true. Grading day."

Chapter Seven

THE CONVERSATION WITH THE WIDOW NEUMANN dried up, so Coble headed back to town. He couldn't figure her out. She'd had a hard life, but this was a land for it. Everyone had a story to tell. It was almost like the killer had done her a favor. A cruel thought, but could the killer have known her situation? Perhaps someone local?

Still in a dark mood, he went back to town on the same road. It was handy, the shortest way, and mighty smooth riding. He took a perverse pleasure in the solitary hoof-prints he left behind. The paint pranced with his head up, enjoying the easy trail and throwing the occasional dirt clod. We all have our small pleasures.

So far, all he knew was the man who killed Hans Neumann was tall, wore dark clothing and a low-crowned hat. If he also killed Jenny, the killer was stealthy and had a penchant for leaving a remembrance. Whether it was a clue or just plain mockery was unknown. Maybe both. And if it was the same man who killed Baby Face, he was a damned fine shot.

Once away from the German settlement, the paint made his way at a slow walk down the churned and muddy street in the new part of town. Through the openings between buildings, he could see freight wagons moving about, keeping the supplies coming and not clogging up the main street for the paying customers. Someone had thought ahead about that. He wondered who was running the New Town. He hadn't heard of a mayor or any local government. If the town survived, that would come later.

It was pushing midday with the hitching rails on both sides of the street crowded with horses and a few carriages. Maybe there was a lunch special somewhere to draw a crowd? He'd seen some lively towns or districts in certain parts of towns, but nothing like this. He'd heard of it, seen it from a distance, but wasn't ready for the way it looked.

There was a crowd on the boardwalks—mostly men with a few saloon girls bouncing from one door to another. He wondered which establishment offered ballroom dancing for the genteel and affluent patrons. Those two ideas always seemed at odds to him. He didn't see anyone who matched that description. Apparently, those folks only came out at night.

A sharp whistle from a balcony caught his attention. A woman in bloomers gave him a bare-chested wave and then broke out in giggles when a man in dirty white long-johns grabbed her around the waist and dragged her inside. Never one to interfere with true love or a paying customer, he looked the other way. Not his business. Not today.

The loudest piano music he'd ever heard started as he passed the open doors of a saloon. Whoever played for Gold's Emporium must have forearms like a lumberjack and the stamina of an Apache runner. Most of the buildings on either side looked about the same, so he took little notice of them. If it weren't for the girl and music, he wouldn't have noticed Gold's either. People and their daily shenanigans look about the same in every town.

Nearing the end of the street, he could see the cottonwoods in the distance. He woke the paint with a jab from his boots and cantered the rest of the way to the grove. The fence-jumping horse stood restless under one of the trees, ignoring the form lying on the ground. The young man was face down in the shade of the cottonwood. A ripping hole punctured his hat that lay cast to the side. Coble wished it still covered the head.

From the position of the body, he couldn't tell what direction the shot came from. The hole in the hat told him it was from an elevated position. His memory went back to another hill...another head-shot. His gaze searched every possible avenue for this shooting to happen and found nothing. Over-hanging limbs would block a shot from the roof of the nearest building. Any of the buildings from farther down the street would be a possibility.

He couldn't believe what his senses were telling him. Could this have been a setup to lure him here —and then commit murder right at his feet? Why? Was the killer like a pet cat that brings a dead mouse to its owner as if to say, *Look what I have done?*

"Mister, raise your hands where we can see them."

Muffled voices and shuffling footfalls of people approaching had registered but he didn't pay much attention. When he turned there must have been thirty people gathered around. It looked like the same crew that graced the boardwalks in town. Maybe this was better entertainment for them. He wished they were sober.

The speaker was a big man in a ruffled shirt. His suit and manner of dress spelled gambler, or maybe saloon owner. Reasonable wasn't part of his look.

"I didn't kill him."

"Mister, you're right next to the body. Seems cut and dried to me. Now, you drop them pistols and raise your hands like I told you."

Most of the group carried guns, and some had their weapons pulled. He had about as much chance as a chicken at a coyote convention. "Boys, my name is Coble Bray, and I'm a US Marshal. I'll not give up my guns."

"None of that means you didn't kill him." The man laughed. "Hell, marshals die real easy around here."

Coble's hand caressed the walnut grip of his

belly gun. For once, the paint stood steady. He didn't like the looks of the crowd, and the circumstance seemed contrived. He hadn't heard a shot. Given all the racket along the street, how could they? How did they know the boy was dead?

He shook his head. A cold knot formed in his stomach, and he started to pull his pistol. They were coming, but he'd rather go out shooting than give himself to the mob. No lynching would happen this day.

"Think about this, people. I had no reason. Nothing to gain."

As the crowd surged forward, a woman's sharp voice cut in. "Stop it. How about we solve this without a shooting or a hanging that you'll all regret later?"

The man leading them looked away with a curse and then answered in a truculent voice. "Who says we'll regret it?"

"Murphy, you ain't got a lick of sense." The woman's voice snapped at him like the end of a whip.

Damned if it wasn't Mrs. Peabody. The group of men stopped, and he wondered what hold or influence she had over them. But it was like Moses parting the sea when she walked through from the rear of the group.

"If you'll allow me." She moved toward my horse, looking over her shoulder at the men. "All we have to do is see if his guns have been fired. Should be some powder on the barrel, and you'd be able to smell it, don't you think?"

Several were nodding at her words, and Coble wondered how many of the men wanted to be there. She looked at him with an expression somewhere between humor and don't let me down.

"Mr. Bray, if you'll give me one pistol at a time, you'll be able to keep a small amount of protection." Glancing at the men and then back at him, she continued. "Although I'd be careful how you do it."

She took the pistols with practiced ease and looked them over. A couple of minutes later, she spoke to the men. "Gather around. This man's weapons have not been fired." She held up her hands. "No powder on me at all. And no spent shells."

Murphy wouldn't let it go. "What about his long gun?"

Coble wondered why the man was pushing so hard. He shucked his Winchester and pointed it at Murphy, making him back up a few paces. "How about you come up here and check it."

Mrs. Peabody held up her hand. "Now, hold on. This little shindig is about over. Don't be stirring it up again. Murphy, get over here and check his rifle." She turned to Coble. "No surprises?"

His gaze settled on her. She stood straight as a post in a gray traveling suit with a small bonnet perched on her head. He noticed her hand was inside her clutch and wondered what it held. A derringer wouldn't help much. He reversed the rifle and handed it to Murphy with his left hand. His right hand remained on the butt of his pistol.

"You be careful with that rifle, Murphy. My pistol has a strange notion that the rifle hates it. If that rifle even points in my general direction, my pistol fires at it. Damnedest thing."

Murphy smirked at him but took the hint. After checking the rifle, he handed it back with a grudging shrug and then headed back toward the crowd.

"Murphy?" The man stopped and looked over his shoulder. "How did you get out here so quick? Why did you think I'd killed this man? From where you're standing, you can't see the body. None of you could."

"You already killed some friends of mine. Besides, we had word of what you did, and the word was to get out here quick before you could get away. He said you were going to kill a friend of ours." His gaze was steady. "Not sure that's still not true."

Coble watched the crowd walking back toward the saloons. Murphy didn't seem to like being alone. "Who told you all this?"

"Don't know, Marshal. It was third hand by the time I got the word."

Murphy walked away, and Coble thought there was uncertainty in his expression, but it may have been wishful thinking. The knot in his stomach was easing but there was a lot of sweat on his brow that didn't come from the hot day.

He sat on the paint until the last of the crowd

was gone. Seems the town folk were predisposed to be against him. Most threw him hostile glances as they left. He noticed the Fallon boy watching from the fringe of the crowd. Would he heed the warning? Someone wound Murphy up tight as a clock spring. He'd seen Dave Sawyer watching from a distance, still wearing his food-stained apron. How'd he arrive so fast?

And a German sitting on a buckboard pulled by a magnificent pair of blacks—staring him down. He shook his head and stared back. Hell, man, it was just a road.

Startled by a hand on his leg, he looked down at Mrs. Peabody. Her gaze held his. "We need to talk. Sooner the better."

She didn't look any different than the last time he'd seen her. Her years seemed to have stopped by sheer force of will. Before he could answer, she patted him on the leg again. "I'll send a note."

This town seemed to be a puppet show with strings pulling people everywhere. Who was the puppet master? Was this all to lure him into a trap?

His attention turned to a buckboard pulling up close to the body. A woman sat looking down, shoulders wrapped with a shawl on a hot day and clutching it tight around her. She shook all over a couple of times and then wrapped the reins on the brake.

He dismounted and walked over to her before she could get down. "Ma'am, do you know this boy?"

Startled, lost in thought, she shrugged and answered with a strained voice. "Near as I can tell, I think it's my son." She gestured toward the trees. "That's his horse. Those are his clothes. His face..."

"I'm sorry, ma'am. What's your son's name?" He thought to get her attention from the horror she was looking at but couldn't see any way to do that.

"Billy Baker. I'm Irma."

He gave her a puzzled look. "How'd you know to come here?"

She looked at him then. "A boy came a floggin' it up on a horse, said a man told him my Billy had been shot and where to find him."

Someone else told to come. Another puppet string. Informed before the boy died. Once again, he scanned the tree line and tops of the buildings. Nothing looked out of place...but then, would he know if it was?

"You sit tight, ma'am. I'll load him up for you."

He rolled the boy in a tarp he found in the back of the wagon, picked him up, and placed him inside. The boy's jumping horse was standing close, so he tied it to the back. When last seen, the young man was full of life and excitement, eager to show off his horse. Now? It was a poor end.

"Where would you like to take him?"

Her shoulders sagged in defeat—her voice was rough and listless. "I'll take him home."

"Do you have a man at there? Someone to take care of the burying?"

"No. Just me." She straightened a bit. "I'm alone

now. My husband died in the mines over at Joplin. They said he dug into some sort of gas pocket and suffocated. I don't even know what that means."

She shook her head. "Billy and I moved out here to get away from the cesspool Joplin is becoming. Guess it didn't make no difference."

Her gaze pinned him, tears making a muddy furrow down her cheeks. "Why did this happen?"

Not how, or who did it—but why? He'd rather have answered the easier questions. So far, he'd found no sense to any of the killings going on. He studied her for a long moment before he spoke.

"I'm afraid there are no easy answers. Even a good one wouldn't ease your pain. There was no sense to this that I can see. None. I'm sorry."

"That's a badge hanging on your pocket. Will you make this right?"

He met her gaze a moment and had to look away, shaking his head. She said they were from Joplin. From the way she talked, the sound of her voice, he'd put her farther south in the Arkansas hills. A land of feud and taking offense at the smallest perceived slight.

"No badge will ever make this right, ma'am. But mark my words. There will be a reckoning."

She turned the wagon toward the road out of town. He followed along, knowing she wanted no conversation—having none to give. It was a peaceful-looking day. Nature has a way of ignoring the people infesting its domain, knowing it can outlast the blight.

He gave a hopeful glance back down the street, looking for Mrs. Peabody, thinking she might be around to give comfort to the woman. She'd disappeared. Just as well. She never looked all that comforting anyway.

———

IT WAS an hour before sunset when he finished burying Billy Baker. It was easy digging for about two feet, then it was pick and shovel work to get through the hard clay. When he stood wiping the sweat away with his discarded shirt, she spoke to him.

"If you'll wait, I'll go get my Bible."

"If you'll allow me, ma'am. I have my own."

She watched as he retrieved the Bible from his saddlebag and put on a clean shirt—clean being a relative term since pulling it from the bottom of his possibles bag.

"Are you a man of God, Mr. Bray?"

"That's a hard question to answer. We're all children of God. But we often lose our way and struggle to find the right road back. We cannot allow the evil in this land to run unchecked. To stop it, one often has to stray from a righteous path."

"That sounds like an excuse."

He stared at her a moment. "I'm not good at offering comfort."

She stood with him at the foot of her son's grave. "You don't look like any avenging angel I've ever dreamed of, but I wish you well. Would you read over my son?"

"I'll do that, and pray for all of us."

After Coble read over Billy Baker, he offered to take her back to town, to be around people. She refused. They were alike in that. He never understood why being in a crowd would help with grief. It always seemed to him people were more interested in watching to see how the grieved took their loss, if they broke down...if they cried.

He left her sitting on a log next to two graves... one old, one new. She was slumped over, looking like the beaten woman she was. He didn't know what to do for her—not for her grief but her physical needs. If there was a church, he'd call on the congregants to help. So far, he'd seen no steeples or crosses in Hard Times, and it seemed people wanted it that way.

———

IT WAS full dark when he walked between the coal-oil lamps highlighting the doors of the livery. After putting up his horse, he mentioned the woman's plight to Fred Curry.

"I don't know, Fred. I didn't get the sense she wanted to keep living. She may still be sitting there in the dark."

The man nodded. "We have a committee of women in the old town that take care of things like that."

Coble nodded, relieved the widow would get some help. "Well, I hope they don't keep too busy."

"Then, maybe you should leave, Marshal."

He glanced at Fred, seeing no animosity, just a neutral tone and steady gaze.

"Why?"

"People are dying. Because of you, I had to kill a man today. Ain't done that since the Indian wars. Didn't like it then. Don't like it now. It ain't all your fault, I get that. But it's all around you—follows you."

In a soft voice, Coble tried to explain. Why do people whisper when there's been a death? The grim reaper already knows where you are.

"I tried to give up the badge. Thought I had it done and didn't miss it. It found me again."

"How does that happen?"

He frowned and gave a slow head-shake, thinking of reasons that seemed righteous on one day and unclear on the next. "I made a bad decision, Fred. We all do that, on occasion. Sometimes the price is high."

Fred chuckled. "Well, don't try to corner the market on bad thinking. Everyone messes up now and again. Besides, there's enough dead people around here already."

The man graced him with a smile—more a grimace, like smiling was unfamiliar. "I appreciate you mentioning this. We'll take care of Mrs. Baker. That was a strange deal."

"You have no idea."

Thankful for the consideration, he made the weary trudge across to the sheriff's office. He didn't light a lamp, just stumbled to the cot and lay down. Drawing a pistol, he kept hold of it while waiting for sleep to take hold of him.

Still no Priest and he was becoming too entangled in the town to leave it for a doubtful home. Who knew if Maria would be there? If Priest didn't show up tomorrow, he'd assume his friend ran into trouble. He could use his help. Chasing down honest killers was one thing. Playing head games was another. He was fast with his gun and a tough man. He knew and accepted that. But was he smart enough?

Someone was killing people just to make sure Coble was there—that he'd see it. It didn't take much to know the killer was playing with him...for reasons unknown. When a cat tired of playing with the mouse it caught, he'd kill it. All he had to do was make the cat show itself before it was ready and survive the meeting.

He got up and put a bar across the door. It didn't look too sturdy, so he wedged a chair under the door latch. Closing the shutters on the windows, he stretched out in the sweltering heat and tried to sleep. Again.

Chapter Eight

COBLE HURTLED FROM THE DREAMLESS SLEEP OF exhaustion and was two steps toward the door before he woke. He was grateful he didn't shoot himself in the foot—or shoot through the door to stop the incessant pounding and shaking.

After he moved the chair and lifted the bar, he stepped through the doorway to find the German road-grader standing there. Coble thought for a moment that this man may haunt him for a fair amount of time.

They stared at each other a moment. The man's eyes wide as he looked at the pistol pointed at his belly. Finally, Coble holstered the gun and broke the silence.

"Well?"

The road-grader tried twice before he could speak. "There's trouble out at the Neumann place. You should come." He turned and left in a display of the worst horse-riding Coble had seen. It was a testament to why he'd always seen the man on a wagon. The rider was an opposing force to every move the horse made. Nothing like the late Billy Baker.

He stood a moment, straightening his clothes and rubbing the stubble on his face—thinking of breakfast. Or lunch. Or a bath and a shave. Maybe he'd get lunch. As he walked toward the livery, Fred came out leading the paint.

"I woke your horse up. That's the sleepiest horse I ever seen. It's a wonder he wakes up enough to eat."

"How'd you know I'd need him?"

Fred scratched his head under his hat. "Saw that square head pounding on your door. Figured something was going on."

"Trouble again out at the Neumann place. That's all I know."

The hat finally jostled off the man's head. He caught it deftly and then looked closely at Coble. "You don't look so good. Most people would be up and through with their morning ablutions by now."

"I'm not a priest." He didn't see any kind of comprehension on the hostler's face, so he continued. "Ablution is a ritual washing of...never mind. It was a rough day yesterday."

Moving to a trough by the door of the stable, he took off his hat and buried his head in the water. Wiping his face and smoothing back his hair, he clamped his hat back on his head.

Fred was grinning at him. "Sorry you had a bad

day yesterday. This day ain't likely to get better. Had a mare piss in that trough last night. Ain't had a chance to change it."

He stood a moment with his eyes closed, thinking of a quiet forest with a stream running over moss-covered rocks, and then wiped his mouth with the back of his hand. It'd been a spur-of-the-moment action to help wake himself up. You can't shoot someone for your own stupidity, even if you want to, no matter how tempting. He spoke after his temper cooled.

"Yeah. I expect you're right. But it is early, and I have all day to change my luck." He checked the cinch and then mounted the paint. "Thanks for bringing the horse and the late warning."

Fred turned and spoke over his shoulder. "You need to pay up. When you die, your horse ain't worth all that much."

When?

———

QUESTIONS PLAGUED him as he rode to the farm. Had the killer come back? Was his fear for Mary Neumann well-founded? When she'd told him about her husband's death and her rape, she'd seemed submissive—almost melancholy about the whole thing. If he came back, did she resist this time? Would she?

Working alone was going against him. He couldn't cover enough ground. What he needed was several people to get ahead of this man—or for the killer to make a big mistake. He urged the paint into a lope and felt relieved someone's tracks marred the smooth dirt road.

When he rode up to the Neumann's place there were several horses standing around and a buggy tied up to the rail. He walked uninvited inside to see the room full of men. No women. Odd.

Conversation stopped, but he doubted he'd understand it anyway. He could see Mary curled up on her bed with her back to the room. Unconscious or embarrassed? Being prone to embarrassment was not the impression she'd given him at their first meeting.

"What's happened?"

A tall man stepped forward. Black seemed to be a uniform they all wore. "That killer came back and hurt her." Most of the group echoed his words. "Why haven't you caught that man, Marshal? How many more must suffer?"

"Who are you?" He tried to brush by the man as he continued toward the bed.

The man's expression appeared affronted as he stepped in front of Coble. "I'm the Elder of our congregation. Jonas Draguemueller."

Coble stared at him a moment, rolling the last name over in his mind. "I'll call you Elder."

"You find my last name offensive?" The man stood straight as a board. His beard pointed straight at Coble, glaring at him past a beak of a nose.

Names are not offensive—mostly. People are.

The amount of time he'd have to spend practicing the man's last name was more than he wanted to spend. Maybe later.

"Nope, just looking for simplicity. I don't plan on knowing you long enough to practice your name."

Striding past the elder, he put his hand on her shoulder. She seemed asleep, or maybe she had her eyes closed because she didn't want to deal with the herd of males around her. Her forehead trickled blood from a cut, and he could see dirt on her cheeks that might be a bruise later. It takes a while for bruising to show up. When he squeezed her shoulder, he felt her flinch away. Not asleep. Fine with him.

He leveled his gaze at the man behind him. "Have you sent for a doctor?"

The elder shook his head. "Don't have one. My people are in danger until you find this man. You should leave and look for him. You've no business here."

"If there is no doctor, who is to care for her?"

"We've tried to talk to her and she won't allow us to touch her. She's headstrong and foolish. Several men in our community have offered her a home. This is what happens to a woman alone. She should know that."

He looked at the elder, trying to decide what all that meant. "So, because she doesn't want to live with you or practice your ways, no one will help her? You're going to stand here and watch her die?"

When no answer came, he pointed to the road-grader. "I don't know your name."

The reluctant answer came as a sullen mumble. "Alvin."

"Do you know Mrs. Peabody?"

"Everyone does." The man paid particular attention to the floor, scuffing a shoe over a splintered blemish.

"Go get her. Tell her what's happened and ask her to come and help."

The man didn't move, looking at the elder.

Coble put his hand on his pistol. "Now would be a good time for you to leave. And Alvin? Take a buggy. I want to see you get there alive."

After the man left, Coble turned back to the elder. "Where's her baby?"

"Well taken care of. She's hurt too bad to take care of it."

"How would you know that?" He stared at the man until the elder started looking uncomfortable. "The baby comes back here. Right now. Understood?"

When the man didn't acknowledge, he tried again. "I don't want to arrest anyone, but you'll be first on my list if you don't start moving. Baby stealing is serious. So is beating the mother."

The elder backed up and nodded to someone. They left in a hurry.

"Everyone outside. Now."

They didn't want to go, but finally emptied out onto the porch and ground beyond. He closed the door on them and turned back to Mary. What had she said about the man who killed her husband and used her? Smooth? Gentle and persistent? This action didn't follow her description. No part of this made sense.

"Mary, can you hear me?" He watched a tear squeeze from her eye. "Who did this to you?"

She tried to turn and gasped from pain, holding her side. Finally, she shook her head.

He gave her an awkward pat on the shoulder. "That's alright, I'll figure it out. You rest easy."

Sighing, he stood a moment and then walked outside. Mrs. Peabody arrived at the same time as a couple of women dressed in gray and black. One of the women held a baby.

"Mary Neumann's been beaten." He stared at the men on the porch while talking to Mrs. Peabody. "Seems there's a lack of proper care around here, or any intent to give it. Will you help her? I'd take it as a kindness."

She looked at him a moment with an odd expression and then turned to stare at the woman with the baby. "Is that her baby?"

Wondering how she knew that, Coble nodded. "Supposed to be."

Staring at the women a moment, she finally nodded at them, and they came forward. She turned back to Coble. "Keep the men out."

As the women entered the home, he marveled that they accepted her leadership in their own community. Not one spared a glance at any of them. Turning back to the men, he spoke to the elder.

"So, who in this fine bunch of men has been trying to get the widow Neumann to live with them?"

"That's none of your concern. A woman needs a husband."

Coble stared at him. "I asked you a question."

The elder couldn't seem to help glancing at a stocky man in a straw hat trying to fade behind the other men.

"So, you think the killer of Mr. Neumann came back and beat up the wife? Instead of killing her? Is that the story you want me to believe?"

He pushed by the elder and pointed to the man. "Step up here."

The man made a show of shrugging and rolling his eyes as he moved to the porch. He stood before Coble with a smirk on his face and his hands in his pockets. He was well set up, looking strong as an ox with muscles bulging his shirt. Probably pulled a plow instead of the mule. Light-haired and blue-eyed, like all the rest. A man with a fresh scratch on his face and mockery in his expression.

"What's the problem, Marshal?"

Before he could reply, Mrs. Peabody stepped onto the porch. "Coble."

He turned, knowing anger made a mask of his face. "Will she live?"

She nodded. "We have her in a chair. If you'll

help me load her in my surrey, I'll take her home with me. You'll need to come with me to help."

He stared at her, knowing there was more to her meaning than she said. "What about the baby?"

"One of these good women is nursing. She'll take care of the baby for the day, or until Mary heals enough to resume care." She looked at the men. "At least the women of this bunch have some Christian kindness."

They loaded Mary onto the buggy, ignoring the gathering. Once situated, the women looked at him. He met their gaze and nodded. They expected something—waited for it.

He walked back to the smirking man. "What's your name?"

The smirk was back. "George."

"George. I won't ask your last name...probably can't pronounce it anyway. But, if she dies, that will be on your tombstone. Under your name, the inscription will be coward."

His eyes shifted from the surrey back to Coble. "Aw, I never hurt her much—"

Coble's fist buried itself in the man's stomach, and then he stepped back to avoid everything the man had eaten splashing on the ground. The man lay groaning in his own vomit.

"I meant what I said. If she dies, I will find you. If my mood turns bad, I may come back for you anyway. There's no place in this world for people like you."

He turned to the elder, who stared with a shocked expression at the man on the ground.

"You lied to me."

The elder looked at the ground. Coble didn't let up on him. "How do you square this with your brand of religion? You tried to hide a woman-beater and condoned his actions. Are you one, also? Should I go check your wife? That's assuming any woman could stand being around you."

He looked around at the men and none would meet his gaze. "Does your God condone this? Is that how you treat your wives? If it is, you'd better start praying I never hear of it."

Coble paused, taking a deep breath. His temper seemed close to the surface lately and that troubled him. Uncertainty of a killer's identity shouldn't color his reactions, but it still hung over him like a cloud.

"You people don't cross me again. Hear this. I am not your enemy—don't make me one. Punish this man according to your ways. See to it. Or, I will."

As he mounted the paint, he watched Mrs. Peabody drive away with the girl. He didn't know what they expected from him—hoped they got it. He'd find out soon enough.

Following the wagon, it was a few minutes of slow riding to arrive at Mrs. Peabody's house. The home was just outside the old town and hidden in a grove of trees, the outside looking well-kept.

Flowers were in window boxes, and the grass was clipped short. He wondered how she did that, not seeing any sheep or goats, when he spied the scythe leaning against the house. He couldn't picture her using the heavy instrument.

He carried Mary into a side-room and lay the moaning girl on the cot. As he covered her with a light blanket, he was surprised when Mrs. Peabody threw it off her.

"You get on out of here. Thanks for the help."

"Think she'll be alright?"

"Probably. Just beat up. I don't know why men always think they can beat on women and get away with it."

He pointed to the thin red line on his cheek. "My wife laid the quirt to me. And she's definitely female."

"Well, I suspect you deserved it. Now go."

———

RIDING BACK TOWARD TOWN, he approached a man carrying a deer over his shoulder. It was a large whitetail, but the man's shoulders bulged with muscle, and he walked like the weight was nothing.

"Can I help you, friend? We could throw that carcass across the back of my horse."

The man didn't glance up. "No. I got it."

"Alright, then. That's a nice deer. And a head shot? Just the one?"

"All I needed."

He rode beside the man a moment before moving on up the road. The man was less than friendly. Not by his conversation but his tone. It said don't bother me. Maybe he was German?

Chapter Nine

WHEN HE ARRIVED AT THE OFFICE, FRED WAS waiting for him. Looping the paint's reins around the hitch rail, he joined the man in the shade of the awning.

"Here's one of them telegraphical messages that come in for you. A boy brought it over from Joplin and was asking around for you. He wouldn't give it to me unless I gave him a dollar." Fred waited with his hand out.

Digging in his pocket, he gave the hostler two dollars. "Thanks. Appreciate it."

One of the coins came flipping back. "I ain't your mailman."

Coble grinned at him. "You like me, Fred. It gives me a warm feeling knowing that."

He watched the man stomp little puff balls of dust on his way back to the stable before he dug the message from the envelope.

"Priest shot. Will pull through. Coming your way. Be careful."

Maria signed the message. What the hell was she doing in Kansas City? Now she is coming to Hard Times? It would have been easier to ride cross-country. Why was she with Priest? He had the awful thought she'd shot him in anger. Stranger things could happen.

He started toward Fred's livery to ask about sending a return message when a woman in a surrey about ran him over. She jumped from the wagon while it still rolled and ran inside the dark confines of the barn. He caught the horse and tied it to a post. Before he could reach the open doors, Fred came out carrying his rifle. The woman was close behind him.

He held up his hand. "Whoa, hoss. What's going on?"

The man skidded to a stop. "This lady and her daughter were coming through the new part of town when some men came out of Gold's and took the girl right off the wagon."

That sounded unlikely, even for this town. "Did they take her back inside?"

The woman nodded, tears running down her cheeks. "Please do something. I can't stand to think what they'll do to her in there."

He met Fred's gaze across the top of her head. This was too convenient. Another setup, and they both knew it. And it was well played because he'd have to go investigate and intervene. He didn't think they'd harm the girl until they knew if he would show up. She'd be safe enough for the moment—if you didn't count humiliation.

They talked as they moved toward the saloon. "How old? What's she look like?"

"She's just an innocent sixteen-year-old, Marshal. Dark-haired like me and wearing a blue dress."

That was a dumb question. If he couldn't tell the difference between a young farm girl and a saloon worker, he needed to turn in his badge—and his eyes. And he wouldn't debate innocence with her. Experience told him that innocence is relative and often differed between what someone was and how society viewed them. He'd seen a lot of innocence lost before the age of sixteen.

"Alright. I'll see what's going on." They were on the shady side of the street, across from the Emporium. "Fred, you stay here. Put the lady under cover. If I come out with my tail on fire, you have my permission to put it out."

He hesitated a moment. "That means shoot them, not me."

Fred checked the loads in his rifle. "I may just shoot everybody. Getting tired of this."

Coble didn't comment on that and, in a few moments, entered the double doors of the saloon. He paused, waiting for his eyes to adjust to the gloom. His head already hurt from that damned piano.

There was a path left between tables through the middle of the floor, with more scattered around in a rough circle. Across the room was a long bar with a brass footrest. At each end of it were two men with rifles. His first thought was they'd have a hard time shooting without hitting several people at once. Considering that a moment, it was a needless worry. They wouldn't care.

Except for the piano, there was silence in the room. All eyes were on him. Some looked with eagerness, and the rest were nervous, probably longing to be somewhere else. He didn't blame them.

Sitting at a table close to the bar, Murphy held a struggling girl. It didn't take much to know she didn't want to be there. The man grinned at him.

Coble made an abrupt turn and walked to the corner of the room, laying his hand on the piano player's shoulder. It was the man he'd seen carrying the deer and built like one of those weightlifters he'd read about. He'd seen men like this lift fifty-gallon whiskey barrels over their head to build strength. Most normal men couldn't pick one up.

The man glanced up at him, still playing. His gaze was flat and dead-looking, like someone coming out of an opium den. His fingers danced over the keys like he was hammering nails.

He patted his shoulder again. "Take a break, friend."

The player turned away and kept banging on the keys. Not in the mood to discuss the situation, Coble shrugged and laid him out with a pistol barrel over his ear. The piano player's face hitting the keyboard played a last discordant chord as he slumped forward.

The silence rippled ahead of him until the barkeep farthest away stopped banging glasses around and stared at him. Holstering his pistol, he weaved his way through the tables toward Murphy.

Ignoring the saloon owner, he kept his gaze on the girl. At sixteen, she looked twenty, and her fresh-faced beauty put most of the working girls to shame. Instead of struggling, she should have been kicking with the heavy boots she wore. That would have been painful.

"What's your name, girl?"

She still fought against the grip on her arms. The look she gave him didn't hold much faith in the male species.

"Macie."

"Well, Macie. You need to hold still for just a moment while I talk to this man. Can you do that for me?"

The girl stopped struggling and stared at him, her chest heaving as she caught her breath. He switched his gaze away from the torn buttons on the front and the white expanse beneath.

"Murphy, you ain't got a lick of sense."

"Well, I am disappointed. You cost me money, Marshal. I lost a bet with the bartender. Told him you were too smart to be caught like this." The man grinned at him. "And I'm the one sitting here with a pretty girl on my lap while you're boxed in to where you can't get away. You may as well admit it. I've got you this time."

Chairs scraped on the floor as people moved away from them. Someone was slapping the unconscious keyboard artist, trying to wake him up.

"So, the other time was a setup? Did you kill Billy?"

"Nope. Like I said, just knew it was going to happen."

"You've got a lot of girls here." Coble looked around a moment. "I'd bet some are younger than this one. You don't need her, she's served her purpose. Now, let her go."

The man laughed, playing to the crowd. "Yeah, but this one is...fresh. Pretty, ain't she?"

Coble's gaze didn't waver from the man. He already knew where the two men with rifles were. But would they shoot into the crowd?

"Kidnapping is a hanging offense, but you won't make it to the rope. I figure your time is up around here. Who put you up to this? Why don't you tell them to come and take the bullet for you? The person pulling your strings is a coward, Murphy. You have to know that."

The saloonkeeper's gaze flicked around, checking his men as a worried look came to his eyes.

It was Coble's turn to grin. "Yeah, you kind of messed that up, didn't you? You had your men positioned to shoot me as I came in the door. Since they didn't, you got a problem. If they shoot me now, they might hit you too. Can't help it. How are you feeling about that right now?"

Some of his bluster came back. "And the girl." His mocking smile fell into place. "She'll be killed if you start anything."

Coble shook his head. "Not going to happen. She's done you no harm and you know it."

Holding out his hand, he spoke to the girl. "Macie, you slide off his lap and don't get between us. Move slow."

The hand gripping her shoulder relaxed and the girl did as he asked, and then bolted around Coble and headed for the front door. When she moved, he saw Murphy had already drawn his pistol, hidden behind the girl. All he had to do was point it.

The smile was wider now. "How's it feel to know you're going to die, Marshal? I'm gonna hang your hat behind the bar for a trophy."

Coble took his hat off and looked at it. "Well, it ain't much of a hat, although the hat band is worth a little something. And I feel about like any other day. Should you get lucky, it would solve some personal problems I have and make more than a few people happy. I can't deny that. But we all die, soon or late. Today may be my time."

The sound of a Winchester levering a shell into its chamber is distinctive, and he knew it was for effect because, in the silence of the saloon, the ejected shell rattled as it hit the floor. Fred's voice carried across the distance.

"Don't you worry none about these other boys, Coble. They're out of it."

With a small smile, he put his attention back on Murphy. "What's it going to be? You're holding a gun, so you got a couple of choices. You can drop it and come with me peaceful. I'll send you to Fort Smith for kidnapping a young girl. I can make a good case for slavery and forced prostitution to spice it up a little. Or, you can try and shoot me."

Facing the angry man's burning eyes, he continued, "You might make it. Makes no difference to me. I'll even give you a target."

He moved with a slow left hand, put his hat back on, and took out his badge, hanging it on his shirt pocket.

"See? There it is, right over my heart. This badge already cost me a good woman and a peaceful ranch life. Some folks tell me it's causing people to die all around it. Maybe it's my turn."

His voice echoed around the room. "You've got a gun in your hand, Murphy. Your thumb is on the hammer and finger on the trigger. All you have to do is cock that pistol and kill me."

A line of sweat trickled down Murphy's forehead. "I got friends. You can't do this."

"Murphy, I don't believe that for a moment. I don't think you've any friends at all that you didn't either buy or intimidate. But I could be wrong. I'll be glad to wait if you want to trot them out. We'll make it a party."

Thinking the man was giving up, he almost

missed it. Murphy relaxed, seemed to slump in his chair, but his eyes gave away his purpose and his right shoulder twitched. Two shots echoed off the walls, one coming a fraction sooner.

Coble took a step back, turned, and walked toward the door, shaking his head. "He missed the damned badge."

Fred stood facing one side of the saloon and Tom Fallon faced the other. The hostler lowered his rifle and glanced at Coble.

"He damned near didn't. We need to get you back to the office. You're leaking all over the floor."

Coble glanced back at Murphy, still shrouded in powder smoke and spread-eagled on his chair. It was hard to tell if the silent crowd cared either way.

"I reckon I'm done here." His glance took in the young man facing the crowd in the saloon. "Thought I told you to leave."

Tom shrugged. "Saw the girl come out and Fred going in. Figured you could use some help."

He raised his rifle when someone moved next to the bar—lowered it when they sat back down.

"Trying to clean my slate, so to speak. And Fred's right. We need to get you out of here."

Coble tried to holster his gun, missed both times. Fred took the gun from him and slammed it home. He stepped outside and was surprised at the crowd. Maybe he was cheap entertainment.

Macie was there with her mother. Instead of thanking him, she stared at the Fallon boy. Guess he has a fan. And Peabody. Where'd she come from?

And they all looked funny. He could hear them but couldn't understand their words. Faces faded to gray. What the hell?

———

He woke in stages with feverish images guiding the way, remembering screaming and pain. That same foggy memory stamped them as his own. Staring fuzzy-headed at the ceiling, he could hear women's voices and a lower grumble sounding like a man. His hand went to his waist, searching for a gun that wasn't there. Wherever his gun went, the pants went with it. At least they'd put a blanket over him.

Grunting from the pain in his shoulder, he swung his feet off the bed and sat up.

"Well, I guess he's alive." Peabody's caustic voice came from near the door.

Searching a sketchy memory, he couldn't think of anything that would make her react that way. Maybe it was just his way with women.

"Where are my pants?"

Her heels clicked on the floorboards as she approached him, a cool hand touching his forehead. "Good. Fever's gone. Can you stand?"

He glanced up at her. "Might. If I had pants."

A low chuckle came from the doorway. Mary Neumann came in, followed by Fred. "Kind of late for modesty, don't you think, considering who's been changing your diapers for the last week?"

"A week?" He glanced around at all the faces grinning at him. "How could I lose a week?"

"You remember Murphy shooting a hole through your shoulder? He must have kept his bullets in that poor excuse of a privy that sets out back. You've been out of your head with fever. Fred lassoed a sawbones from Joplin and dragged him over here to see to your wound."

The old hostler grinned at him. "Thought I was going to get to sell me a horse, if I could wake him up."

"Don't act so disappointed. Maybe you'll have better luck next time." He moved his shoulder. "Doesn't feel too bad. Mighty sore, though." He paused a moment. "And sticky."

"We been putting honey on it. Mary said it'd keep the infection down. Looks like it works. The doctor said you were lucky, like we didn't already know that. The ball passed through clean, except for taking a notch from your shoulder blade. He said in another week, you should be in good shape."

"Obliged, ladies. You've done me a kindness." He rubbed his stomach, looking around. "I could eat."

Mary snorted. "Just like a man. Wants his pants. Wants fed. Next thing he'll be wanting a woman. Although that order does get reversed on occasion."

Before he could form an answer, Fred came in with an arm full of clothes. "If these witchy women will leave you alone enough, you can get dressed."

Mrs. Peabody turned as she and Mary went out

the door. "When you're dressed, we need to talk. Some things have happened."

"More killings?"

"Other than Murphy?" She held her palm out, maybe startled by his expression. "No, just things."

———

A FEW MINUTES LATER, he was sitting at the desk tearing into a plate of eggs and potatoes. He had a room full of people staring at him. "What? I haven't eaten in a week."

Fred shook his head. "You get eggs on that new shirt and I'm going to be unhappy."

Coble looked at the man a moment. "I haven't known you all that long, but you've been unhappy the whole length of it."

He finally cleaned his plate with a piece of bread and started on the coffee. "So, what's going on in town?"

Fred and the Fallon boy were standing by the door. Peabody and Mary were sitting on the bed, Mary idly swinging her legs back and forth. One thing he noticed right away.

"Where's the baby?"

She didn't look concerned, smiling at him. "Wet nurse. Handy."

He sat back in his chair. "So tell me."

"We've been taking a walk through town several times a day with rifles. Everything has been quiet since you killed Murphy. That kind of quieted down the riff-raff."

"With that long-range shooter around, that seems risky."

Tom spoke up. "I go from door to door, stay close to buildings and such. Mix things up a little. Fred comes behind me, so if I go down or get shot at, he'll at least be able to fire back and maybe see who's doing it."

It was a tactic fraught with problems, but many a lawman had done the same thing. "You like being a target?"

The young man laughed. "Not so much."

Coble thought a moment. "Well, it's up to you. It's your town. Run it any way you like. Have a meeting with the town founders and make it official. I'll try and stay out of the way."

"That's all there is to it? Appoint ourselves and go to work?"

"Yep. Of course, you need to remember that, unless you're appointed by a judge, you can get unappointed just as easy."

When the men left, Mrs. Peabody came in again, pulling up a chair beside the desk. She sat in silence, staring at him, hands folded on her lap.

He passed a hand over his face while he watched her. "So, who shaved me?"

"I did, among other things." A small smile turned the corners of her mouth. "There isn't much about you that I don't know."

They stared at each other while he thought

about what she knew. He noted a large kettle on the stove and a basin close to the bed, sitting on a small table. Towels were drying, hung on nails driven into the wall. He wasn't aware nursing was one of her skills.

"Thank you. My wife should have been here to take care of things like that. Since I'm feeling good, I must be in your debt. Your nursing skills are appreciated." He met her gaze a moment. "Very appreciated."

She chuckled at that. "Oh, it wasn't all me. Mary helped some."

He could feel heat starting to rise from his collar. From the size of her smile, she was enjoying his discomfort.

"Well, thank her as well. Was there anyone else I need to thank? Perhaps a long-suffering women's society to parade through the door?"

Her smile was quick, but then sobered. "It's not that good of a show. You're kind of beat up for a man your age."

"Tell me something I don't know. Any other news or useful tidbits?"

She gave him a curious look. "Like Fred said, there have been no more killings. I find that odd."

He glanced away, watching dust-balls floating in the sunlight shining through the window. "Not so odd when you think of it. They did the killings for my benefit. I don't expect there to be any more while I'm laid up and cannot respond."

Mrs. Peabody shrugged. "No one has taken over

the town after you killed Murphy. It seems the ownership of all the buildings in the new town is cloudy. Best I can find out, it's some consortium from Joplin."

At his surprised look, she glanced away. "You talked in your sleep, so I've tried to find answers. I agree you were set up with Murphy, especially since he tried to get you lynched when Billy was killed."

"So, what else did I rave about?" He was starting to re-think his statement about feeling good.

"A lot of things I don't have answers for, like the actions of your wife. She sounds demented, if not downright cruel. Of course, I don't have her side of the story, and I can understand her anger when you took up the badge again."

"It probably saved her the trouble of inventing something else. The quiet life was chaffing her."

"And you're not so straight-laced yourself. Poor Mary had to leave the room a few times." Her gaze locked on his, along with a mocking smile.

He laughed at that one and then winced as pain lanced through his shoulder. "You're making that up. I can't imagine Mary being surprised by anything at all."

"You'd be surprised. She's not as worldly as she puts on."

"Good. I guess. Not all of us should be jaded by life. Although a little worldliness might keep her from making mistakes." He gave her a quick glance. "Not that it's helped me any."

She watched him a moment, and he could tell

something was coming. "I've a story to tell if you care to listen."

He smiled at her. There's always a story. "Seems I'd better listen. You might not feed me again."

She started in a soft voice. "There is a story of a man during the late affliction that was a most uncivil war. This man was a mercenary, selling his skills to the highest bidder. It seems someone figured out that it wasn't the generals that made a difference in the conflict. It was the leaders that carried out the orders, whether they were officers or enlisted."

She hesitated, lost in reflection a moment. "Men that were good at leading soldiers in battle and displayed exceptional tactics seemed to die at an alarming rate, and not during battle. All killed while riding between camps or resting in peaceful places. Guess how they died?"

He nodded, already knowing the answer. "I'd guess head-shots from a long distance away."

Nodding, she continued. "Men would state they didn't hear the shot. From what I found out, the shooter didn't care much which side he worked for —just the money. And he always managed to leave a calling card."

At his questioning look, she answered. "Sometimes. Or something else that might be important to those viewing the body."

He nodded, guessing where the story was going. "So, how did that gain your interest?"

Her straight shoulders slumped a moment. "My

husband was killed that way. He was a dashing young lieutenant who swept me off my feet at the tender age of fourteen, before he went away to war. One of his superiors told me they didn't need to give him orders, just pointed him in the right direction and he took care of it. He was a good man. A good leader."

"I'm sorry for your loss. You were awfully young to have to deal with that. But everyone lost something in that damned war."

He thought a moment and then caught her gaze. "You seem to be a fount of information on a lot of things. Are you sure you weren't a spy in the late conflict?"

Her eyebrows rose as she gave him a level look and made no effort to answer. A slow smile formed as she watched him. Fifteen years ago, she'd be discounted by most as a combatant, young enough to make it hurt where it counts—old enough to know when and where to use her talents. He looked at her with a new understanding. Intelligence often wanes with age, in her case, it did not. And there were hundreds of female spies during the war and afterward.

"Well, I'll be damned."

Her voice was mocking. "Oh...we're all damned, Mr. Bray. It's the matter of redemption that is the problem."

"Pinks?"

She inclined her head in a short nod. "For a short while. And then the Federals."

"Like Maria."

Her face lost expression as she sat back, her mouth slack before making a perfect oh. Of all the things that had happened, something finally seemed to surprise her. When she didn't say anything, he continued.

"So, what now?"

"It would seem the man you're looking for is the one I'd given up finding. I still don't know who he is. When he killed that man a year ago and left a cross with him, I decided to stay right here. How we continue is unclear. All I can do is keep listening and watching."

Her parting statement left him with a chill. "Coble, you seem to be the honey tree that attracts that particular bear, at least until he tires of you. Maybe we can make something happen. If you feel up to it, there is a dance next week. Would you meet me there?"

A dance? Maybe that would pull out all the players. Everyone would attend, if for nothing else than to see who else came. Maria had refused to come with him, so he'd offer companionship for the dance —that was all.

"How can I refuse such a delightful lady. Is it an invitation to have some fun or be shot at?"

Her gaze held steady on his. "Stir the pot, Mr. Bray. Stir the pot."

When she left, he searched the drawers of the desk and found some blank paper and a pencil. He thought to write down what he knew of the killings.

Maybe that would help point him in the right direction. He was lost in thought, staring at the paper, when Fred poked his head through the open doorway.

"Just seeing if you're...what'cha doin'?"

Coble looked up from his exercise in futility. "I'm trying to find answers to questions I haven't thought about."

The hostler stared at him a moment and shook his head. "Uh-huh. That sounded like you're speaking English but I didn't understand a word of it. You better go back to bed. That fever may be coming back."

———

IT WAS a quiet week before the dance. Coble started sitting under the porch in front of the office. Heat with a breeze was better than being inside the stuffy office. He had the constant care from two nurses and moved about under the watchful eye of Fred. It was a good feeling to have friends.

But he knew what was coming, and so did they.

He was walking with Fred when they passed by the butcher shop. There was a steer in the chute, culled from the holding pen. A man walked up to the animal and dropped it with a blow to the head from a beanbag, or sap as some called it, usually a pouch filled with lead pellets.

Tying a rope around the hind legs, a simple block and tackle raised the animal off the ground.

He pushed a bucket under the head and cut its throat. Simple and efficient, with no wasted effort.

They were walking on by when Coble saw the deer and called to the butcher.

"Who shot the deer?"

The man looked at them a moment. "Don't remember."

"Mighty chancy shot, shooting it in the head."

"Word is, this was a thousand-yard shot. Easy for the right man." The butcher shrugged, his expression guarded as they backtracked. "Probably lying, most shooters do. And a head shot? Depends on how close you are. Or, maybe he wanted the hide with no holes in it."

Fred was looking at him. "Why the interest in a dead animal?"

"Seems odd. You ever see a dear killed that way?"

The man snorted, wiping his hands on a greasy apron. "I've seen them shot everywhere. Saw one shot in the butt once. The man trailed it for miles before he got a kill shot. Why?"

"Just curious. It seems out of place. You ever see anyone around with one of those sniper rifles they used during the war? It'd have a tube on top to look through—long barrel. Or maybe a long-barreled Sharps."

Fred thought a moment. "It wouldn't be that old Whitworth rifle. It's still a muzzle-loader, and we could always tell who was shooting them by their black eyes. It had a hell of a kick, and that tube would hit them right in the eye. That's not counting the black powder."

"Not a brass shell." Coble nodded. "So, a Sharps then. Still...few men keep those around anymore. Most favor the Winchester."

"Don't seem like the kind of gun a man would be carrying around anyway. Those long barrels are kind of awkward."

He nodded. "And noticeable. I wonder where he hides it?"

"Hides what?"

Coble laughed. "Pay attention, Fred. Stop watching the women hanging over the rail over at Golds. The rifle. A man killed last year with a long shot, and then Billy Baker the same way? That rifle has to be somewhere." He continued, watching Fred stumble while watching the show on Gold's balcony. "And I still wonder who shot that deer."

And then he remembered the piano man.

Chapter Ten

WHEN COBLE ACCEPTED MRS. PEABODY'S invitation to the weekly dance, he decided to spring for a new broadcloth suit. The dry goods store next door just happened to have a rack full of them. Remembering the sign on the door of the dance hall reading *Formal Dancing, No Range Clothes Allowed* and comparing it to the lettering on the sign above the suits, he could see free enterprise at work. Create a market and then supply the goods. There was a lesson in that.

A portly woman named Sadie took him in tow, measured, poked, and prodded, and finally came up with a suit that fit. It only took her minutes to let out the cuffs for his long legs and take in a hitch or two at the waist. The coat fit right off the rack. Satisfied, he shook hands with her as he left, looking for a barber and a bath. Neither was available, so he settled for creek water and shaving in front of a cracked, fly-speckled mirror in the office.

Paying for the suit made him realize that Judge MacGregor neglected to mention his pay and, more to the point, when he'd get it. The town of Hard Times had a lot of buildings popping up, but a bank wasn't one of them. The risk of frequent and forcible withdrawals was too great a risk.

The dance hall was a sight to see and rivaled establishments in Kansas City. Several chandeliers hung from a high ceiling, and oil-burning lamps graced the surrounding walls. Feet covered most of the polished landscape of hardwood. The long dresses kept it swept—shoes kept it buffed. A four-piece band situated in a corner tuned up their strings along with a piano. The piano man from Gold's played softly with the strings. He didn't know the man could be that light-fingered.

Before he went inside, he paused to look around, if for no other reason than to ensure himself he was still in the same country and looking at the same dusty thoroughfare. The street was lined with horses standing hip-shot, surreys and buckboards seemingly parked by a drunken chess player, and men in bowler hats escorting crinoline ladies toward the door he blocked for the moment.

On the other side of the street were saloons, men in rough clothing, and women selling a good time—some hanging over upper-story railings with little clothing on to offer anyone a chance to see their wares. Real life on one side, genteel fantasy on the other. Would there be soiled doves on this side of the street? The only admission price was a pretty dress. And once you change the packaging, how do you tell the difference? Knights or knaves, ladies or courtesans. Shaking his head, he passed through the door.

Tables circled the walls, leaving the center open for dancing. He was surprised to see Tom Fallon sitting with the girl they'd snatched from the saloon, along with Macie's watchful mother. Mary Neumann was at another table, surrounded by several suitors—still dressed in black. Was black part of her mourning process or simply highlighting her blond curls? He wondered what the elders in her community thought of that situation, and that brought his first smile of the evening. A smile because he really liked the her, liked her mettle. He knew she had her life well in hand and would be doing alright in the future.

Judging by the number of unattached men lining the walls, the ladies would have scant time to rest between dances. It was a time for the women to trot out what finery they had and show off a bit, and no one begrudged it. Men would take a back seat this night—at least until alcohol-induced jealousies made things interesting. Claims would be made and rights disputed. Prizes would go to the winners of an ageless process to weed out the weak and the slow. This was life brought together in a crowded room to be studied or danced around.

Mrs. Peabody sat at a table with a couple of men engaging her in conversation. They cast dark looks his way when she looked up and invited him to sit.

Her soft voice couldn't compete against the background noise, so he moved close while grinning at the men. They shrugged and wandered off, looking for easier pickings.

"My, you're a handsome man tonight."

While some women wore hoop skirts more suited for a formal ball held by the Joplin elite, she was soft in deep-red silk and lace. Her hair was down and curled in a casual look. He'd been around women enough to know it took her hours to achieve that. Somehow, she'd thrown off that older-woman appearance. Maybe it was the dim lighting, but a curious thing.

He gave her his best bow and kissed her hand. "And you are a vision of loveliness. I'm stunned by your transformation."

The band started playing a waltz. Leaving his hat along with her handbag to save their table, they took to the floor. She proved to be a weightless dancer in his arms. She leaned up with a breathless whisper.

"Call me Kate. It will be more appropriate... later."

He chuckled. "You have a first name? I'm shocked."

As they glided around the floor, navigating between the other couples, the worry of unsolved murders faded away, and he relaxed in the simple exercise of the dance. Maybe that was the intent of the dance organizers. Gambling and gaming were stressful occupations and needed relief. When the band took a short break they stopped by the punch bowl on the way back to the table. Dancing was thirsty work.

After sitting, she spoke again. "I'm glad to see you're not drinking whiskey tonight."

He looked at her a moment and raised his cup. "The punch suits me, although it has a strange sweetness. Someone may be doctoring it a little. And just so you know, I will not dance better using the hard stuff. Quite the opposite. Why the concern?"

Her grip was tight on his arm. "Please do me a favor and hold your temper. And yes, I know you have one. Some things may happen tonight that you won't like. You should stay calm. With your shoulder, you're in no shape for fighting."

His hand came up and rubbed his shoulder. "Now, I've never seen a good dance without a few friendly altercations. Too many unattached men and too few women. Besides, it's part of the entertainment. More to the point, why do you think I'd ruin your evening with brawling?"

"Well." She gave him a serious look. "For one thing, Maria is here. I got the impression your relationship is contentious."

He looked around, thinking the good times were about to end and feeling more than a little guilty for dancing with another woman.

"We didn't part on too good a note but we can fix that. How do you know her?"

"I talked to her earlier at the dress shop and told

her you might be here tonight. Women can't help but talk." She laid her hand on his arm, staring up at him. "She's not alone, Coble. Be prepared for that."

Not alone? That set him back a little. He didn't know what to expect—but not that. "Well, it is a dance, and for the record, I'm not alone either."

Something in her tone gave him a queasy ball in his stomach. He started to ask the obvious questions when he saw her eyes tracking someone approaching their table. In that moment, she reminded him of a cat watching mice—tail twitching with watchful eyes, contemplating the next meal.

For the first time in weeks, his wife was before him. Maria wore an emerald green dress that was tight where it mattered and left little to the imagination. He hadn't seen a dress that low-cut since the girl in the saloon across the street leaned over to advertise her wares. Her dusky skin looked flushed, and her shining, black hair was combed high and held with an alabaster comb. A matching necklace graced her cleavage with a pearl pendant. She still took his breath away, and he hoped she couldn't see the hurt in his eyes—hurt from something that might now be beyond fixing. And Kate was right. She was not alone.

Coble's standing was abrupt, a disjointed move making his chair slide and thump on the floor. Maria flinched, holding her palm out. For the life of him, he couldn't tell if it was to touch him or hold him away.

Her voice was tremulous. "Coble, it's...it's good to see you."

He couldn't help it. The bile of frustration was rising fast. Good to see him? That was cold. Close as she was, there seemed to be an icy wall forming between them.

"Really? That's odd, considering our last conversation. You seemed in an almighty hurry to get rid of me."

He gave the man with her a quick glance. This was uncharted territory, and he didn't know how to act. In his mind, once you're married, the competition with others is over—yet here he stood with Kate, doing the same thing... sort of.

"Now I'm beginning to see why you wanted me to leave."

She took a step back, and the familiar anger flashed in her eyes. Holding the arm of the man next to her, she interrupted. "And you say that while sitting in the company of another woman? Once again, you are clueless. By the way, this is Oxford Graham. He's a dear friend."

He hadn't paid much attention to the man until she introduced him. As Oxford held out his hand to shake, Coble glanced at it and then met his gaze. "And just how dear a friend are you? I'll confess to never hearing of you. But then, I'm only her husband. It seems my wife has secrets."

The man's extended hand died a slow death in the air and clenched into a fist, dropping down to his side. They stared at each other for a moment of mutual dislike before the man spoke.

"I have heard you're a rather goatish, uncouth, and barely civilized ruffian better suited for the range than mingling in this genteel company. Maria's description of you was right on the mark."

Coble almost smiled. Almost. "Did you practice that phrase? You did, didn't you." He glanced at Maria, and her gaze dropped. "Perhaps I am all she says. Thinking about it, I probably am. And you can add foolish to my list, because I was. But I'm at least honest. Of course, I haven't known her forever like you, but I am surprised she prefers such foppish friends."

A giggle erupted from the table and he glanced at Kate, remembering his promise. Wide-eyed, she had a hand to her mouth as if she surprised herself.

He turned back to his wife. "Have you made up some sort of story to tell me of your past? Something to reconcile this? Oh, and not to be forgotten, how's our friend Priest?"

"Priest is recovering, but it's slow."

For a moment, she looked like the old Maria, and then her hands started wringing a stylish cloth he supposed some called a handkerchief in more uncouth circles.

"Coble, we need to talk. Things have happened."

His shoulders rose along with his eyebrows. "Now you want to talk? Funny. I didn't get much chance before."

"I'm sorry about that." She glanced at Kate. "Please? Perhaps we could have some privacy?"

Kate started to rise. "Shall I dance with your beau?"

"No," Oxford interjected. "There's no point in putting this off."

Taking an envelope from his coat pocket, he handed it to Coble. "It gives me great pleasure to present this to a lout like you. According to Judge Colin MacGregor, you are no longer married to Miss Santos. Since this is an annulment, the marriage never happened. You may go away now. Frankly, I'm surprised they let you in the door."

Coble leaned slightly on the table, thankful for its support. A body blow couldn't have hurt more as he struggled to understand. His gaze slid to Kate, who held an odd expression as a tear coursed down her cheek.

"That's strange. I remember days and nights that cemented our union. In that endeavor, we christened a lot of furniture. On what grounds could you possibly have this done?"

Maria put her hand on his arm. "Coble, please let me explain."

"Explain?" He jerked his arm away, unable to keep the bitterness from his voice. "I'm sorry. I don't know what to call you now. If you're not my ex-wife, how shall I address you? If we weren't married all that time, what name should I use? What's a proper title for someone who does this to their husband? Give me a hint. Perhaps the women across the street could offer a name for you. At least they are honest about their profession."

Her gasp was sharp, but he'd at least wiped the anger and mockery from her face. Her legs gave out and she sat awkwardly in a chair.

He turned to Oxford. "What's your stake in this? Has she been keeping you on the side just for fun and recreation? Was a month married to me a restriction she could not bear?"

The man's smile never reached his eyes. "Oh, we've known each other for years—since an exciting time in New Orleans. When she discovered I was around, she looked me up. Being a lawyer, I presented her case to the judge. He agreed with me and thought this solution would free you to pursue your vocation. Hunting deranged killers, of all things? Kind of like putting a fox in the hen house, don't you think?"

"And how did she discover you were sniffing around?"

For some reason, that question was bouncing around his gutted brain. Were they passing notes like school kids, or using their vaquero as a messenger? None of it made sense.

"Oh, I've heard a lot about you." The man continued, pausing for a moment, shaking his head. "Maria says you can walk in a room, look around, and point to a ne'er-do-well and pronounce them guilty. She's told me of this—this talent of yours. You just glance around and point out a killer. She doesn't know if you're like a Cheyenne medicine man or a voodoo witch doctor from New Orleans. But it seems to scare her."

Coble smiled and shook his head. It was a little like taking a bullet—a grunting moment of pain and disorientation. He could still feel the pain, but his mind started working again.

"I doubt anything scares her. And there's no magic involved. Nothing like that at all, and it doesn't always work." He glanced at Maria. "It's obvious that I get fooled a lot when things are too close to me." He glanced back at the man. "Do you like music?"

"Of course. I'm very educated."

"Very?" Coble rolled his eyes. "No doubt you are. Then think of it this way. I look for discord, like bad poetry that strains to rhyme. People trying hard to hide often exist in syncopated time—they just don't fit. And then the kicker is that they often tell me, in their own way. They feel superior and can't help themselves. Kind of reminds me of you."

He caught the man's gaze and smiled. "Now, why would that be?"

"I don't understand." The man shrugged. "You mean they dare you to catch them?"

"And by doing so, they put themselves at a disadvantage. The onus is on them, not me."

Oxford's expression was cold. "Unless someone kills you."

He locked his gaze on the man, nodding. "Unless they kill me."

The man's voice mocked Coble. "It's too bad so

many things have happened to you. Seems your run of good luck has ended. I'm surprised you can function after all your failures. I mean, look at you. Someone has been making a fool of you, killing people at your feet—leaving clues well beyond your ken. Now, it seems someone has stolen your wife from under your nose. And to be honest, it didn't take much."

Maria's voice turned anguished. "Oxford!"

He continued, ignoring her outburst. "You don't inspire a lot of loyalty, do you? And you'll pardon me if I'm not impressed with your legendary skills. Seems to me you've lost everything you hold dear. What possible reason could you have to keep on living?"

Coble shrugged, a small smile forming as he glanced at Maria. "Murder and clues? Sounds like somebody's been talking out of school, among other things. I always thought information passed between a man and his wife was sacred. So. Fooled again. That's getting to be a habit. Besides, I'm not out to impress. And as for the...lady, you can't steal what's not mine. The fact that you're here means she was never mine. I don't know what her game is, but I'm not included in it. I suspect I never was."

The lawyer gave a slight bow along with a satisfied smirk. "Well, then. Since you seem befuddled, and not likely to think your way out of it, I think our business here is done. Maria?"

He held out his hand to her, still watching Coble. "It seems your lovely wife...oh, I'm sorry...

Miss Santos is an exquisite dancer, and I intend to enjoy her charms for the rest of the evening. All of them."

Oxford hit the floor with a thump, shoulders first. Stupidity comes in many forms. His was in gloating on his conquest. Coble's was in spreading blood across the man's face with his fist. Music covered the sound, and his landing went unnoticed in the sea of gliding and stomping feet. The piano man was getting his second wind.

Maria helped the lawyer up and wiped at his cheek. He gave Coble a bloody smile. The look in his eyes made Coble back a step as he stood watching, rubbing his knuckles. They moved away, Maria casting a glance over her shoulder while being propelled along with a hand on her elbow.

Kate cleared her throat. "Seems you've forgotten me while this little drama was going on. Not very chivalrous of you, Coble. And you broke your promise."

Tearing his gaze from Maria's retreating form, he sat heavily next to her with a sigh. "Sorry. I was a little distracted."

She scooted closer to him. "I know. But you should understand that all is not as it seems. There are games afoot."

Games? He shook his head. "I'm in no mood for that. I should call it a night. Being polite is tiring, and I'm not much for games."

She shook her head, curls bouncing in the light. "No. You cannot be by yourself. In your mood, you'll go right out and shoot someone. I'll not let that happen."

Tapping an ivory and lace fan against her lips, she gave him a pensive look. "As a better choice, would you consider escorting me home? There are dangerous people about, and I feel unsafe. We could have a nightcap and maybe a late dinner, if you're interested. I'm sure you'll find the menu quite extensive."

He drew a slow hand down his face, sighed, and then looked at her with a small, slow smile. "Kate, there are two sure things in this world. Death and stupidity. Do I look dead to you?"

Her laugh was low and throaty as she pinned him with her gaze. "Well, I'm glad you didn't ask that of me a couple of weeks ago. It was a tossup. And the idea isn't as stupid as you think. In my opinion, you are very much alive and need this. You need to step away—re-think and re-group. Trust me on this. If you get too close to a problem, it surrounds you, and it's hard to get away."

He glanced toward the dance floor but felt a hand on his cheek pulling him back around. Her lips were moist and parted, the soft light of candles shone in her eyes. There was a heady smell about her. Not perfume, but one that gave beauty to any female—the alluring scent of arousal. Was it because of him, or the violence? Thoughts of Maria still pressed against his mind. He couldn't move past his anger and bewilderment. Why did she annul the marriage? The merry-go-round of emotion made him dizzy until, finally, anger won.

And why not? Fidelity was a yoke he'd put on himself, a complication not shared by his wife...or whatever she was now. An acquaintance? Dalliance? Mistake?

Tapping the folded document on the table, he leaned over and whispered. "It seems I'm unattached with no marital responsibilities at all. I doubt if I'll be good company but thank you for the invitation. I find myself hungry."

———

HE LEFT her neatly furnished cottage the next morning before dawn, satisfied he'd tasted all she had on the menu. Pausing at her threshold, he glanced back. He'd found her secret. Her age was nowhere near what she made herself up to be. She was young and vibrant—an unexpected turn of events. There was just enough light to see her sprawled in exhausted sleep on tussled sheets. He'd worked through a lot of anger, and she'd been a willing surrogate. Since she wasn't awake to tell him, one could only assume he'd purported himself well. Seems he had a need for her kind of cookery. And once again, she was right.

He closed her door and heard it latch.

The question was...why her masquerade? Who was she fooling? And an even larger question. What madness caused him so much guilt for taking her home?

Chapter Eleven

THE SUN STILL HID BELOW THE HORIZON WHEN Coble's attention drew to the lanterns burning outside the café. Stepping inside he saw Fred Curry and Tom Fallon sitting at a corner table. When he walked toward them, Fred looked up with big eyes and a slack expression and then grabbed for his pocket watch.

"Tom?" Fred pulled out a pocket watch and waved it around. "This is history in the making. Right here in this room. Look at this. The sun ain't up yet, but this man looks like Coble Bray."

Concern furrowed a line between his brows. "Why are you up so early, Coble?"

The same lady he'd talked to before brought a pewter mug and filled it with coffee, giving him what passed for a pre-dawn smile. "Getcha something?"

He nodded. "Fill up a plate with whatever you

have this morning and keep the coffee coming. And thank you, ma'am."

The two men were grinning at him.

"What?"

"Been working up an appetite?" With a wink at his partner, Fred resumed digging into his own breakfast.

The plate of whatever-you-have arrived before he could reply and Coble grabbed a fork. The food smelled good, and in fact—he was hungry.

He pointed a fork at them. "You boys ending the night or starting the day?"

Fred's good humor left. "Been a long night. After you left the dance, someone filled the punch bowl with whiskey. I expect you know what happened after that. They don't call it skull-buster for nothing."

"Sounds about normal for a country dance— after all the gentle folks leave, of course."

Tom smirked at them. "Well, they did keep it friendly after that. They didn't kill anyone, and after a few cuts and bruises, things were peaceful. So, what are you doing out and about so early?"

Coble scraped up the last of his eggs, potatoes, and mystery meat and sopped the gravy with a thick piece of bread.

"Going to take a ride. Maybe go back to the ranch for a couple of days. I have some powerful deciding to do."

Fred shook his head. "You can't leave yet."

"Why not? You men have things under control."

"That ain't it. Your horse won't wake up for another hour. If I get him up too early, he's cranky."

He told them about his last horse, Red. "Now that was a cranky horse. He'd buck, stomp, and bite. I was never sure if I hated him or liked him."

"Why ain't you riding him?"

"He was a good horse and always got me where I needed to be. We were riding a thin trail around a rocky slope and he caught a rattlesnake bite on his nose. I still think he tried to bite the snake—he did kill it. I wound up sitting in a pile of brush."

They sat, remembering good horses and bad. Fred couldn't stand the silence. "Did he make it?"

Coble shook his head. "No. His nose swelled up and he couldn't breathe. Wasn't anything I could do. You know? There were times I wanted to shoot that horse just on general principles...but not that way."

"When he died, we were less than a mile from home. His last ride and he got me home."

He paused a moment. "He was a good horse."

————

Two hours later, Coble led the paint out of the stable barn. He was nursing a sore foot and the horse seemed to grin through the bit in its teeth. Maybe he imagined it, but the horse had a funny look in its eyes. Was Red in there someplace?

————

HE STOPPED at the same cottonwood-enshrouded stream he'd camped at before. Since it was late evening, he decided to stop rather than push on and putter around in the dark at the ranch. No telling who, or what, had taken up residence there in the last few days.

Better prepared for the trail this time, he had fry-bread and bacon sizzling over a small fire. He'd picked up a three-legged contraption from a miner down on his luck that suspended a pan over the fire. He could raise or lower it by a small chain attached to a windlass crank. Handy.

A coffee pot sat on a flat rock, nestled on the edge of the fire. This time, there were two field rats to keep him company, waiting patiently for the bread to cook. All he needed was a few more animals and he'd have the start of some children's fable complete with rainbows and winged horses.

Shaking off the melancholy after the meager meal, he stirred around, finding a likely spot for his bedroll. The paint snorted once, ears up and nose pointed into the darkness. Coble stepped into the shadows next to a tree. Hoofbeats sloshed through the creek and then stopped.

"Hello the camp." The voice was non-committal, like nodding to someone on the street.

Taking the loop off his pistol, Coble stepped out from behind the tree. "Come in if you're friendly. If you're not—take your chances."

The rider came slow into the camp, hands at chest level, reins in his right hand. The man's pistol was on that side showing he was friendly, so far.

He stepped into the light. "Light and set. You're welcome to leftovers if the mice haven't carried them off."

When the man stepped off the saddle, he ground-reined his horse and chuckled. "I've fed a few of those rascals myself."

He paused a moment, watching Coble. "Now, I'm going to reach into my vest pocket and get a paper. I've come to deliver a message, and then I'll be on my way."

The man looked familiar, but Coble couldn't place him. It seemed an odd way to pass a message. The paint wasn't interested in anything but the campfire, not looking out into the night. He nodded to the man.

"Make sure that's all you do. I'm going to assume you're alone?"

The man nodded. "I am. If there's anyone else about tonight, rest assured they're not with me. My name's Faraday, and if I was hunting you, I'd not need help."

Serious or bluster? The rider looked too old for needless bragging. "Heard of you. How'd you happen to get this message?"

"I'm a livestock inspector headed back to KC for my next assignment. A man overheard me talking about it to a bartender and asked if I'd deliver this to you. I assume you're Coble Bray? You fit the description."

He had a moment's thought of how that would be. Tall? Short? Ugly, grumpy-looking man?

"So, what's the message, Mr. Faraday?"

The man stepped forward and handed over an envelope. Coble stuck it in his pocket.

"Did you read it?"

"Nope. Not my style, it's still sealed. I do wonder how he knew where you were going." He paused a moment. "We're both professionals so a small warning. I wouldn't trust anything in that letter. My sense of that one is he's polecat, through and through—and I saw him write the note."

Coble nodded to him. "Thanks for that. I think I know who it's from. A foppish-looking gentleman and a pretty Mexican woman with him?"

The man grinned. "Well, not sure what foppish means, but he sure was a dandy. Does everything like he's watching himself in a mirror. And if you want to call a beautiful woman just pretty, that's your choice. Although I didn't get the sense they were together. I couldn't get much of a read on her, but I'm like most men. I can only judge what a woman tells me and pray she's not lying. They are a breed apart."

Tapping the envelope in the palm of his hand, Coble said. "You're welcome to the fire. It's getting late."

"Naw. Thanks for the offer, but I'm betting we'd both sleep better if I moved on. I'll have the moonlight another hour or so."

Faraday paused a moment. "One thing, though.

The deal with Murphy in Gold's saloon? Why didn't you just walk in there and shoot that peckerwood?"

"It's a point well taken and would have saved me some grief. The girl was in the way. When she moved away, Murphy already had his pistol in his hand, so I was playing for time—for an edge. Never got it, couldn't talk him out of it, so we had to play things out.'

"And you still beat him." Faraday shook his head, smiling.

Coble tapped his wounded shoulder. "Not really."

The man stared at him a moment and then mounted his horse. "So, you say. But he's the one sprouting daisies."

"I doubt that man grows anything but cockle burrs."

Faraday laughed and tipped his hat. "Good day to you, Marshal. Hope you're on the mend."

He stood in the shadows, listening to the horse and rider moving through the brush. It was a sad world when two men couldn't trust one another out on the trail, but Faraday was right. And he'd heard disturbing whispers about the man skirting the law on occasion. But don't we all. On occasion.

Soon, the only sounds were night birds and tree frogs—maybe a rat complaining of a belly ache. Satisfied the man was gone, he added a few sticks to the fire and opened the envelope. It wasn't a long message.

Don't worry about dying. I got your woman and that's enough for now.

He thought long and hard about Oxford Graham. If he was the killer, why did Maria take up with him? He assumed he'd already gotten Maria in a biblical sense, so what did *got your woman* mean? Was she still alive? Rushing back wouldn't change anything. He said a prayer for her safety. She'd spurned him in the worst way, but he didn't hate her. Could not hate her. But the question remained. Why?

————

MID-MORNING THE NEXT DAY, he made it home. As he topped the rise and looked at the ranch buildings below, the horses in the corral didn't alarm him. He had a good idea who the new tenants were. Smoke rose from the chimney of the house. It was a peaceful scene, and he missed it—missed being able to relax. When on the trail or in an unfriendly town, he was on edge and vigilant by necessity. That wore a man down.

Dismounting at the front step, he flinched when the vaquero appeared like a wraith and took the reins for the paint. That was a surprise, but no more than the horse following the man like a docile puppy. Comparing Maria and the paint, it was his gift to always bring out the best in women and horses. A true gift.

With a sigh, Coble stepped inside to find

another surprise. He expected to find Pete Santos sitting at the table. He knew Maria's father would show up sooner or later. It would be an even bet whether he was there to shoot him or offer to help. They'd been partners on several hunts, so maybe he'd get the benefit of the doubt.

The surprise was Priest sitting next to him, looking pale and drawn, served by a young Mexican woman. Brown as a nut with sleek black hair and laughing eyes, she reminded him of someone who left him behind in anger...but fixed his lunch. He stopped inside the door.

"Priest? Seems we've come full circle."

Stepping forward so they wouldn't have to get up, he shook their hands. Pete was reluctant but finally offered. He expected that. "It's good to see both of you."

Pete didn't waste any time. "Where's Maria?"

Sighing, settling in a chair, he pulled the annulment paper from his inside vest pocket and handed it to him. The old puncher stared at him a moment before reading it. It wasn't a long document. Shaking his head, he tossed it to Priest.

"Annulment? And signed by MacGregor?" Priest settled back, leaving the paper on the table. "I would never have expected that. I don't think it's possible given the circumstances since he'd have to have the cooperation of the church. Probably null and void."

"Coble?" Pete's voice was a soft rasp. "I trusted you to take care of my girl. What's happened?"

Irritation colored his reply before he could stop it. "Yeah, like you ever had control of her."

He shook his head, raising his hand to stop the man's reply. "Sorry, Pete."

It took but a few moments to bring them up to date from the time Maria kicked him out to the present. "So, there it is. A group of saloon bums came to move me out of town, and that didn't end well for them. Two more innocents are dead. One a young man who was just a messenger to draw me to a spot. Someone killed him just before I got there, and a mob was already set up for my lynching. An old marshal's badge left on a dead German farmer—his wife raped. Afterward, I had a brief discussion with a man saloon keeper named Murphy. That, too, was a setup. I put him down but took lead in my shoulder doing it. Complicated doesn't begin to describe things, and I'm real tired."

Priest patted his side. "If we were cats..."

Coble agreed. "I know. We're running out of lives. How were you wounded? I can't see you getting into a bar fight."

"Wasn't anything like that. A shot from an alley. Unexpected, to say the least. I was not vigilant."

Pulling a cloth from his pocket, Priest spoke softly. "Before we get too far along."

A silver cross fell out of the handkerchief. "This is the real reason I came. We were resting, hoping to make it on into Hard Times in a day or so."

"Who?"

"You won't believe it. Judge MacGregor and his

secretary. He died, and the assailant beat her terribly before...well, she must have resisted. It wasn't pretty."

Coble sat with elbows on the table, hands steepled in thought. "I wonder if someone wanted you out of the way since you were supposed to come to Hard Times and help me? Who would know that?"

He glanced at his friend. "Didn't Maria come to visit you?"

Priest shrugged. "I heard her voice once, but I wasn't sure. I was in and out a lot."

"The woman was there and cried for you." Juana's voice was soft and then hardened. "I was glad she left. She had no place there."

She blushed when the men turned to stare at her. Her gaze was on Priest, her eyebrow raised, mouth grim in a straight line before she spoke.

"One hen is enough in your house. You don't need more."

"She was a friend, no more. I officiated at their wedding." Priest smiled at them, spreading his hands. "The little one has a possessive nature."

"There's more." Coble took out the message delivered the night before, passing it over to Priest.

"A man named Faraday brought me this note. Said he saw the man write it—Maria was at his shoulder, watching."

Priest regarded it a moment. "You know who wrote this?"

"Now I do. Compare the writing."

Coble continued. "A man named Oxford Graham. I'm sure he wrote them both."

"Do you think...?"

He took out the message left for him a year ago and the one left with Jenny's body. "He's made his mistake."

Priest put them all side to side. His eyebrows rose, and Juana gasped as she peeked over his shoulder.

Pete moved the papers around with his finger, turning them as if a different angle would change the message. "So, what now? How you going to fix this, Coble?"

He shrugged and pulled his hand over his face. "One of the reasons I came back was to clear my head, try to get things in order. It's hard to understand how one man can do all this. There are too many people being influenced...and all against me." He reached into a pocket. "I put pencil to paper before I left to help figure this thing out."

Priest took the paper. Looking at it, he met Coble's gaze over the top.

"It's blank."

Coble gave him a grim smile. "As usual, you have a keen grasp of the situation. But since Faraday delivered the last message to me, things are clearing up. Now the wild card isn't the killer, it is Maria."

The girl came and nudged Priest with her hip. "More coffee?"

He watched the byplay and gave his friend a slow grin. "Your helper seems well entrenched."

"She is my nurse, among other things—hardly left my side." Priest turned and watched her walk back to the counter. "She has helped me realize I didn't love Jenny, though I mourn her loss. Juana has been a rock when I needed help."

He grinned at us. "She's very strong for her size and hard to resist when you're tied to a bed."

Coble laughed. "You realize that's how old Pete got lassoed. Seems to be a pattern."

He raised his hand. "No explanation needed. Everyone needs a nurse, time to time."

The girl gave him a grateful look.

"Back to Maria." Pete wouldn't let it go, and Coble didn't blame him. "Who's this Oxford Graham she's taken up with?"

Coble shrugged. "Don't know him. He seems quite the dandy, likes to throw Shakespearean insults. Not very well, though. I've seen better on the stage. He seems to be someone from her past. Maybe from when she was a Pinkerton."

Priest picked up the thought. "I wonder...if she met this Oxford fellow and mentioned our plans?"

"Not Maria. She wouldn't do something like that. I'm sure you have enemies. Anyone could have shot at you." Pete's voice faded.

"Wasn't there someone that said the simplest explanation is usually the right one?" Juana stood leaning against the sink, drying her hands on a towel. "Could that be the case?"

"Your nurse appears to be educated, Priest."

Coble glanced at him. "You may not be able to escape her clutches."

Priest's voice was soft. "Too late."

"Well, I only see one thing wrong with her." He watched as Juana moved toward them. "She blushes too much."

Pete stood abruptly and walked outside.

Watching him, Coble shrugged. "He's mad at me for losing Maria. I don't blame him, but she didn't give me much choice. This has been out of control since you brought me that damned badge."

Juana sat at the table with a cup of coffee. "So, who is this Oxford Graham?"

He glanced at her, then at Priest. "Oh, I know who he is. And now we know what he is."

"I'll take care of him." Priest's voice didn't have the ring of strength. "I owe him."

Juana's face started to turn red as she stared at them.

Coble shook his head. "No, my friend. You're not up to it yet. I can tell by looking at you. Why don't you stay here until I get back? Let your nurse have her way with you—in a manner of speaking."

His gaze was on his friend as he smiled. "You need to be fully recovered before you start any more adventures. And I may need you later."

"His adventures are over." Juana's voice was firm. "He'll need all his strength for chasing children."

He laughed as he watched them, Priest looked stunned, and her face a study in determination.

"I'm sorry, Juana. He can try domestication, but soon or late, the apple stares up at the branch from whence it came."

Juana stared and then shook her head. "Does he always talk like that?"

Priest nodded. "Sometimes it is worse. The bad part is I understand him."

"As do I." Her lips thinned as she glanced at Coble. "That does not make it true."

———

PETE SAT in a rocker when Coble walked out on the porch. His voice was a low rasp. "How'd you lose her, Coble? What in hell happened?"

He leaned against a post, watching the dust swirl in the barn lot. Low voices came to him from inside —not angry, just conversation between two people comfortable with each other.

"I don't know, Pete. I took the badge. That hurt her more than I could have imagined. But there had to be something else. She was getting bored staying out here. I could tell that. I've never figured what set her off. The next time I saw her, she handed me the paper. It's just one more mystery."

"You need to fix it."

"No. You know me, Pete. Better than anyone but Priest. When she took up with that dandy, whatever covenant we had between us was broken."

"So, you'll throw her away?"

"I cannot throw something away once it has left my hand. I'll protect her if I can, but there are things going on that I know nothing about. Half the time I think I'm just a spectator at a play, waiting for the surprise ending."

Priest came to the door, leaning on Juana and holding the frame with his hand. "You're making a mistake. That's never been your way, Coble. I can tell you're confused. Why are you doing this? You're thinking too much."

He held his hand up to stop Coble's interruption. "If you were at a poker table, you wouldn't play how the card sharps wanted you to. You'd play your own game. You're letting the situation with Maria confuse you. Her motivation has nothing to do with the problem."

He paused a moment as Juana tried to get him to go back inside. "Here's some clarity for you, Coble. Forget their games. They're meaningless. Go back to that two-bit town and start stomping snakes. I wish I could help you. Be yourself. That's all you need to do. Stop second-guessing everybody and making mysteries where none exist. Like Juana hinted at—make it simple. You need to break bread with the devil. Then spit in his eye as you walk away."

Pete's voice broke as his voice cut in. "Just take care of Maria if you can."

Coble shrugged and nodded, gazing across the prairie. "If I can. She's doing things I can't understand, Pete. And she's made her bed with dirty sheets. Some things cannot be undone."

Juana looked up at Priest. "Again?"

"You'll get used to it."

Chapter Twelve

THE RETURN TRIP TO HARD TIMES WAS uneventful. Same heat. Same country. Riding harder than he should have, he didn't stop to feed the rats under the cottonwood. Coming into town, a small tavern caught his eye. His shoulder was sore from the riding. Something wet to slake his thirst and then find something to eat? The hot weather and dusty trail dulled his senses, and he didn't second guess it. The place was clean of trash all around and the boardwalk swept. Maybe the food would be clean. On impulse, he tied up to the hitch rail and went inside.

Caught in a Shakespearean play, the gods were laughing at him. Pausing inside the door, the first thing he saw was Maria standing by a table in the corner. What ill-gotten luck would lead to this? Still, they saw him as he came in, so walking away didn't seem right. He gave himself a rueful smile and shook his head.

He walked to the bar, keeping Maria and her new beau in sight. Graham was gambling while she looked over his shoulder, leaning against him. The gambler was immaculate in a white shirt with garters on the sleeves and a black vest. Maria was... he turned back to the bar, stopping that thought in its tracks.

"What for ya?" The barkeep was a portly man with mutton chops and a dirty apron. The bowler hat perched on his head sported a dent, and a fly crawled on the un-lit cigar in his mouth. Coble tried not to stare but was unsuccessful. The man ignored his scrutiny.

Given the circumstances and company, it was no time for drinking. "Got sarsaparilla?"

The bartender shook his head, frowning around the dead stogie. His voice was an irritating rasp. "Don't carry that crap in here. Have to go clear to Joplin to get it."

He rubbed his hand over his tired face. Hell with it. "Well, what about a shot of skull-buster?"

The cigar nearly fell from the slack jaw. "You like that Indian whiskey? We just keep it around for when cow-pushers get too drunk to notice. No use wasting good likker on them."

Coble shrugged. "I developed a taste for it. Can't decide if it's the gunpowder or strychnine in it. Maybe the soap. I never have to worry about worms, though."

He turned to survey the room, ignoring Maria as she tilted her head toward the door. A warning?

Watching her, he didn't see a man dressed in range clothes stop in front of him.

"You that marshal folks are talking about?"

He glanced in the mirror to see if a sign reading *idiot* hung around his neck. Why did he stop here? He thought for a moment about leaving, but good decisions weren't a part of this day. Coble sized the man up. Dressed in typical trail dress, complete with leather chaps on an impossibly hot day, a stained-gray hat pushed back on his head, and thumbs hooked in his belt. The man looked just drunk enough to get himself in trouble.

"I don't know, friend. I rarely listen to people talking." He turned back to the bar.

The cowboy pushed him with a finger. "Heard you was real tough."

He glanced over his shoulder at the grinning cowboy. "When I have to be. Mostly I leave that to the young squirts like you. Lately, I'm just a big fuzzy kitten. I like to curl up in the sun and warm my old bones."

The man looked around, grinning at his audience. "I bet I'm faster with a gun than you. I been practicing."

A quick glance showed the man's pistol nestled in a simple holster with a loop over the hammer and worn too high for anything but an awkward draw— all serviceable but nothing fancy. This was a working man. Coble looked at him and shrugged.

"Yeah. I'm sure you are. But I wouldn't bet your

life on it. Some good men have said that speed is fine. But accuracy is final. You might think about that."

The puncher still didn't move, so he tried again. "Look, son. I'm not going to shoot you, and I'm too old and tired to let you give me a beating. Have a drink on me and let it go."

When the puncher didn't move, Coble looked past the man at his friends. "Get him out of here. He's drunk."

Another voice spoke up from down the bar. "Don't worry, boys. Marshal Bray ain't much for stand-up fights. Anybody can make him back water."

The bartender set the glass of Indian whiskey on the counter and walked away. Wondering if the day could get any worse, Coble looked at the end of the counter at a man he'd only seen once. But his reputation was known. You'd always find him hanging around looking for a quick dollar. Stages robbed, men sandbagged and rolled. And he always seemed to have money. If any marshal had a to-do list, this man would be on it.

He couldn't side-step this. The next marshal to confront the outlaw might be someone with farmer's hands looking for a way to feed his family. This was his snake to stomp.

"You going to take up that job, Sanibel?"

Sanibel stood with an arm around a dusky bar-girl who was looking for a better place to be.

"Hell, it don't take much of a man to take down a marshal. You boys are a dime-a-dozen and dying like flies down in the Nation."

The noise in the bar dropped to nothing. Past the gunman, he could see Maria with her hand held to her mouth. He wished he could study her eyes to know if she was excited or scared for him. He doubted the latter. And if she cared for him at all, she wouldn't have switched horses.

The piano man keyed up a rousing medley of unrecognizable music. That it carried from a few doors down and across the street was no surprise to him. That man could pound the keys. A chair groaned as someone's weight shifted, punctuated by a nervous cough. A man wearing a miner's cap came through the open doorway into the bar, saw what was going on, turned on his heel, and left with a muttered curse.

With a sigh, Coble turned to face Sanibel while keeping an eye on the drunk. "Are you that man, Sanibel? How much of a man does it take to kill three innocent men?"

The gunman's voice exploded. "What are you talking about?"

Coble stared at him. "You rode up to three good men from the Bar M. They were sitting around a fire drinking coffee at the end of a hard day chasing cattle out of the gullies and thickets. Just minding their own business. Like most decent men, they invited you to share their camp. When you got down from your horse, you just up and shot them. Then you sat by their fire and drank their coffee, ate their food, robbed the bodies, and rode off."

The outlaw started to say something, but the drunk cowboy interrupted. "Sounds like you were there, Marshal."

"Nope. I was not. But a good tracker was. Man's name was Jonas Clyburn." The woman beside Sanibel stiffened and gasped. "He's another one of us dime-a-dozen marshals working in the territory."

The drunk interrupted again. "I heard of him. Ain't he one of them black marshals?"

Coble nodded. "One of the best men on a trail I ever saw, including the Apache."

He looked straight into Sanibel's eyes. "And one of the men wasn't dead when Jonas found them. He named the killer."

"You're lying. That was a fair shooting. They were all wearing guns."

Coble kept staring at him and then shrugged. "As am I."

The girl tried to get away, but Sanibel grabbed her and pulled her to him. "Hold on there, blackie. This won't take long."

As the girl came back to him, Sanibel drew his gun.

Stepping to his right to clear the girl from his line of fire, Coble fired one shot, striking Sanibel in the head. It was the only shot he had in the crowded room. The man fell like a puppet with its strings cut, arms thrown out, and his legs bent at impossible angles.

The girl stood wiping blood from her face with a blue handkerchief. It had white-lace trim, and he thought it was a waste to ruin such a beautiful piece of cloth. She waved it at the gun smoke drifting around them.

With the noise of the gunshot echoing in their ears, the drunk cowboy's voice was loud in the silenced room as he turned to his friends.

"I ain't that fast."

Boots clumping on the wood floor, arms draped over shoulders, the group moved toward the door. For a moment, their four-man parade tried to get through a one-man opening—but they made it.

The girl skirted Sanibel's body and came up to him. "You know Mr. Clyburn?"

Coble nodded. "Met him out in Graham County. Good man. Good marshal."

"He's done a lot for our people." She stood looking at him and he couldn't read her expression.

Her voice was low and husky. "A word of advice? Watch your back. I saw money change hands." Her eyes flicked toward the corner and then settled on Coble. "Or, I could be wrong. Who knows?" With that, she turned to leave.

That wasn't an unexpected piece of news. This whole town was a setup.

"What's your name, girl?"

She looked back at him and rubbed her thumb

and fingers together. "Whatever I'm called by someone holding money, but mostly Josie."

When she turned away again, he called to her. "Hey, Josie? Thanks."

Her eyebrows raised in question.

"For the little bump that put Sanibel off balance. You didn't need to do that. I might have lost that little contest, and then where would you be?"

"Same place a whore always is, Marshal. Under someone's boot." She gave him another look that he couldn't decipher. "You got friends around. Don't forget it."

His gaze traveled over to the poker table. Maria stood looking out the window, standing hip-shot with arms folded and leaning on the sill. Oxford was gathering cards and didn't look happy. The players around his table had vacated for parts unknown. He looked at Coble with that superior smirk, but things were different. Coble knew him now. He was the discordant note—with some hold on Maria.

Coble nodded toward the body. "Friend of yours, Ox? Sorry, but whatever money is on him goes to the undertaker for expenses. No refunds."

Ox came half out of his chair before settling back. "My name is Oxford. And no, I never knew the man."

"That's funny. I thought he was just your style. Did you pay the drunk cow pusher too? Or, just Sanibel."

His eyes reminded Coble of a lizard—lifeless,

never blinking. Maria watched them, her hand in her purse.

Oxford seemed to relax back into his chair. "I don't need to hire anyone. When it's time, you'll find out."

Why the message? Did he think Coble wouldn't recognize the handwriting? Just a taunt in the game of cat and mouse? Coble smiled at him.

"I got your message. It was the last piece of the puzzle. Thank you for that."

Oxford's jaw went slack a moment before he recovered. "I don't know what you mean."

"What message?" Maria's voice came low, tempered by anger.

He smiled, keeping his gaze on Oxford. "Seems Ox sent me a note to say the game was over and I was safe, at least for now. He already had the prize he wanted."

Coble's gaze lifted to Maria. "He had you."

"You going to arrest me for stealing your woman, Marshal? There a law against that? I'd like to see how that warrant is written."

"Oh, there won't be a warrant. It's just a matter of taking care of business. I think now would be a good time, don't you? Your game is over. I know who. I know what. I don't know why, but it doesn't really matter. I think we should settle this right now. That way, I can send a message to Fort Smith and tell them to scratch two names from their list."

Two men came in, unaware of the byplay, grabbed Sanibel's body by the legs, and dragged him out a back door, head thumping its way over the threshold. The bartender scattered sawdust over the blood stains. Except for the stench of black powder, it was like the shooting never happened.

Using the distraction, three men moved through the door and stood waiting, facing Coble. Although dressed differently, they may as well have been peas in a pod. Tied-down holsters and wide-brimmed hats pulled low over their eyes. If he'd grabbed someone off the street, told them he was casting a new play and needed gunmen, this is what they'd bring back.

"Where do you find men like these, Ox? Is pay for honest work around here so small these men follow you around?"

His hand caressed the butt of his pistol. "You'd think they would take the loop off their pistols before coming in."

He held their gaze. Two smiled, knowing his intent. But the third was sweating and moving his hand toward his gun.

"Mister, you move that hand another inch and I'm going to shoot you." When the man stopped, Coble shrugged and continued. "What's it going to be, gentlemen?"

The staring match ended when Maria moved between them and marched out the door. Oxford Graham made a show of it, moving slow like he didn't want to go, but he left. And his three body-guards. None of them spared him a glance as they left.

Coble gave a sigh of relief as he reached for his drink. He'd tried to push it but didn't really want a shooting. The time would come.

He glanced at the bartender. "Sorry about all this. Hell, all I wanted was a drink and a little polite conversation."

"Mister, this place has been called a lot of things —polite ain't one of them."

Chapter Thirteen

IT WAS ONE OF THE FEW TIMES SHE WAS ALONE. Oxford said he had an appointment. Maria locked the door to her room at the boarding house with trembling fingers. She then wedged a chair under the knob. It wasn't foolproof but would slow someone down a moment—sometimes a moment is just enough.

Looking at herself in the mirror, she pulled pins from her hair letting it cascade around her shoulders. Coble Bray. Just like the man. While everyone was playing games, trying to fool one another, he'd cut through all the distractions. She knew that look of his, and it wasn't remorse from killing Sanibel.

He'd found the killer and thought it was Oxford Graham. But there was more. Something didn't fit and she couldn't figure it out.

Sitting on the worn bedspread, she clutched her stomach and reached for the bowl on the dresser—got herself under control and took a deep breath.

She had to come up with a plan to protect Coble. The killer would not fight fair, he'd give no chance.

She'd tried to distance herself from her husband. She'd met Oxford in Kansas City. When she went to see Priest, he'd walked up to her. It didn't take her long to suspect he must have shot Priest, deliberately not killing him, knowing she may show up. A setup.

From that point on, she lost control. He stayed one step ahead of her. What she couldn't understand was why? Why the charade? What didn't she know that would tie it all together? Combing out her hair, she realized she smelled like a cheap cigar or bawdy house floozie. Glancing outside, she realized it was getting late. She needed a bath. It was time to stop this and go to Coble—if he didn't shoot her on sight.

———

COBLE LED the paint to Fred's livery.

"Back already? Must have done some quick thinking."

He shook his head. "The decisions were made for me this time. It's a good thing. Thinking hasn't been one of my better habits lately."

It took a few moments to tell the story of the notes and murders. Fred knew most of the story and nodded.

"I'm not surprised. What now?"

"Spread the word. Let people know what he is—

what he has done. Get it out in the open. He'll either run or come out shooting. Either way, I'll be waiting."

Fred gazed up the street a moment. "Were you ever a sailor? I always wanted to do that. Just take off and let the wind decide where I end up."

He gave the hostler a curious gaze. "Never had the pleasure."

"There's an old saying, red sky in morning— sailor take warning."

"It's afternoon, Fred."

The man pointed up the street. Maria was marching down the boardwalk toward Coble's office.

"Storm coming. I'm going to hide in the barn."

He grinned at the old man. "We're friends. You have my back, right?"

"Course I do—from the barn."

When Coble entered his office, she was leaning against his desk, arms folded under her breasts. It hurt just to look at her. He stared a moment before finding his voice.

"Can't say this is a pleasure, but I'll try and be civil. What can I do for you?"

She stood and put her hand on his arm. "We need to talk."

When he stepped back, her hand fell to her side. "I don't think so. You seem to have made your position damned clear."

He watched as she took a deep breath and

controlled her anger. This was new. Usually, she let it fly untethered and raw.

"Then, I have a story to tell. One we should have talked about a long time ago. Will you at least let me do that? For old times' sake?"

How could she? The night of the dance, she'd seemed intent on pushing him away. Unbidden, his hand went to his vest pocket and pulled out the annulment papers, holding it in front of her face. On the outside he felt like Moses holding the Ten Commandments. Inside, he was close to losing the Indian whiskey.

"I don't have a lot of good memories or have much feeling for old times. I don't have it in me."

She snatched the papers from his hand and tore them in half, throwing the sheets in his face. "Dammit, Coble, sit down and listen."

Her expression softened as she pointed toward his chair. "Please."

He sat, grateful for the reprieve, staring at her. He hadn't felt this wobbly-legged since being wounded—unsure if it was anger or dread. Finally, he waved for her to go ahead. She didn't start where he imagined she would.

"It was that damned key. It wasn't a clue for you and Priest. It was a message for me. A summons. Oxford Graham had found me."

"And the cross? What was the message in that? Why kill Jenny?"

"He's playing a sick game. Lives mean nothing to him. And then he added the key after the undertaker had her ready to ship home. Oxford knew Priest would see it and tell you about the murders. He figured I'd see the key and know what it meant."

He stared at her a moment, his voice came in a rasp. "A message from your long-lost lover?"

"I know you think that, and I'm sorry." Shaking her head, she continued. "I'd been sent to New Orleans shortly after the war to get information about guns being smuggled out of the seaport. The Federals didn't want another insurrection. That led me to Oxford."

She held up her hand when he tried to interrupt. "I left him and returned to Washington, only to find he'd played me for a fool. All the information I got from him was useless. It was embarrassing, but I put it away, thinking that part of my life was over. I decided to come west to see my father. You pretty much know my history after that."

Her gaze held his for a moment before sliding away. "One of the reasons I left in a hurry, and I mean a big hurry, was that I found out he was a killer and I was afraid I would be next. He killed... often."

"Like me?"

Her head shook in a violent tossing of curls. "You have reasons for what you do, it's sometimes necessary. He just...likes it."

Coble thought about it. Nothing was adding up. He still had to be too many places at once.

"Ever see him shoot a long gun?"

She gave him a curious glance. "No. Not ever.

He uses a sleeve gun or a knife. He's a city boy, not likely to use a rifle."

The writing on the notes matched. Faraday saw him write the note. That was enough. But if he didn't use a long gun? Coble had never seen him with a rifle, but that didn't mean much.

They were silent a moment. He could feel the old familiarity of sitting on their porch enjoying the quiet of late evening. It brought a longing that was hard to put down.

He prodded her once more. "The key?"

"You won't like this." Her sigh was long and drawn out. "I'd given it to him as part of the seduction—tied the ribbon on it myself, from my dress. It was to my boarding house room."

She was right, he didn't like it. Not at all. "How do you...square...all of that?"

She shrugged, looking at him with soft eyes. Begging eyes. "Exciting, young, stupid, take your pick. I'm not proud of it...now. I made excuses then."

Shaking his head, he tried to make sense of it and then realized Juana was right. The simple answer was often correct. "New Orleans was no place for a single woman."

Her gaze was sad, watching him work it through his mind. "Don't pick at the scab, Coble. It will serve no purpose."

He didn't acknowledge her voice, staring out the darkening window. Fred was lighting his outside lanterns and piano music carried on the wind—hard sounding, at odds with a peaceful evening.

"I've heard Pinkerton women called whores. Never believed it."

Her voice caught in a sob and a gasp. She shook away tears, determined to see this through. "That's rare—although pillow talk is one of the oldest methods of gleaning information from someone."

Her gaze caught his as she smiled. "I expect the widow Peabody knows everything there is to know about you by now. Don't you think?"

"That was—"

"Different? Because you're a man? A dalliance I'm sure. Still..."

He forced a smile. "I have no wife, no encumbrance at all."

She pointed to the floor at the scattered pieces of paper. "Seems you do. The judge is dead, and so is the witness to the signing."

"You knew of this?"

"He told me the judge fell ill. Knowing him, it didn't take much to figure out anyone else connected to it would also fall ill."

He nodded. "And Ox? I still don't know why you went to him? Why didn't you tell me what you knew right away? That's the hardest part to understand."

Hesitating, she leaned against the desk. "I was shocked. Desperate. It wasn't my best decision, but I did it to protect you. I was afraid, Coble. Still am. You don't know him. He's evil."

"So, you don't think he's killed anyone here? Yet?"

Maria thought on it a moment, going over everything Coble had told her. "I didn't. But now, I don't know. Nothing fits. Maybe we should go talk to Mrs. Peabody. She's good at this kind of thing."

She gave him a hand up. "I'll check your back door is barred and meet you outside."

———

AS HE STEPPED out on the boardwalk, Coble turned at a sound behind him, thinking it was Maria, and felt a numbing blow to his right shoulder. He tried to get to his pistol with his left hand but it was knocked away. He stood helpless, facing a man in shadow—a man wearing the blood-stained, leather apron of the butcher.

He watched the man advance toward him again, the same man he'd watched kill a beef cow the other day with one blow from the sap—a simple contrivance of a leather pouch filled with lead pellets. Killing without leaving a mark on the victim.

The butcher seemed in no hurry as Coble backed away. With no feeling in both hands, there wasn't much he could do but run. Yet his feet seemed mired in the street as he watched the expressionless man raise the sap for the final blow.

A shot turned the man away a moment. Wounded in the stomach, he moved toward Coble again until another bullet hit him in the chest. The butcher went to one knee and finally fell over into the dusty street.

Coble was nearly blinded by the muzzle flash, but his vision cleared fast enough to see Maria still pointing her pistol at the man on the ground. He stared at her. With that one intervention, things had changed, like the hour hand on a clock when it ticked twelve. Moments before, his life had been his own. He could risk it or throw it away. Now, more than before, someone else lay claim to it. Not by a contract signed with ink or words said before an altar. It was a debt signed with blood, and the reason lay dead at their feet—a nondescript man who'd stayed unnoticed until the call to murder came.

Maria knelt by the dead man, moved his apron aside, and emptied his pockets. It was a good thing she wore gloves because a couple of silver crosses spilled out, along with matches and pocket change. The light winked off one as she held it up to Coble.

"Careful touching that cross. I guess I was supposed to be another victim." He looked at her. "When someone killed Mr. Neumann, his wife was raped. Do you think that was the plan here?"

How could she smile at a time like this? She stood and shrugged. "Not by that man. From the way Mary described it, he's too short. It's safe to assume he didn't know about me being inside."

An averted murder and his life was saved, but it left more questions than answers. There are times when the world turns and everything that was old vanishes—when the world you know changes and you can't tell if you've changed with it. You just watch as events pass you by like the hands of a Seth Thomas ticking away.

His breath came ragged as he looked at her. "Not that I'm complaining, you saved my life. But why did you come to me this evening? Why aren't you with your lover?"

"Oh, Coble." She shrugged. "You needed to know certain things, and earlier, I told him to go to hell."

Her face turned to him. "I'll admit he was not happy about that. And my lover? It was a charade. He likes girly boys and it made him ashamed—until the need hit and he went looking again. Joplin is his new haunt. There isn't anything you can't buy there. As for me? He liked to keep a pretty girl on his arm as a distraction. I don't know what made him come west, he should have stayed in New Orleans."

"He came all the way to Kansas City because he liked to hang you on his arm while he walked around? So you could lean on him while he played poker? Makes no sense, Maria. I don't buy it."

Enough feeling was coming back to his hands that he could wiggle his fingers. Boots clumped on the boardwalk as someone drew near.

Fred skidded to a stop, holding up a lantern to survey the dead man. "Dammit. You killed the only butcher in town?"

"Maria didn't like the way he cut meat."

"Glad I don't keep a horse for her." He glanced at Maria. "No offense, ma'am."

No one thought two gunshots were an oddity, so no crowd gathered. Or no one cared. Coble was still trying to lift his hand above his elbows.

"Fred, do you know anything about this man?"

"Nope. Called himself Jones. Might as well been Smith or Gomez. Just showed up one day and started hanging meat. Made a smokehouse out of an outbuilding and started curing ham."

The pain in his shoulder wasn't helping his mind. "Just like that?"

Fred was a man who couldn't talk without his hands, and the lantern weaved a pattern punctuating his reply. "Yeah, just like that. Just like Sadie showed up with a couple of wagons, took over a building, and set up shop. Just like that sky-pilot took over a building a few months ago and tried to start a church. It burned to the ground, but he did try. Just like you ripped off the boards that barred this door and made it into your office. Just like that."

"I really meant when did he show up?" Coble held his hands up in surrender—surprised himself that he could do it. "Let's go over to his place and see if there's anything to tell us who he is, where he comes from?"

Fred handed him the lantern. "Try not to burn the place down, I'll get the undertaker—funny, he just showed up too."

———

THE BUTCHER HAD one room he used for living quarters. It smelled of rancid meat and musty clothes. A fire flickered in a pot-bellied stove to guard against the evening chill with a pot of beans sitting on top. All they found useful was a letter addressed to a Thaddeus Jones from a mail-order place in New Orleans concerning knives suitable for slicing meat. There were animals kept in stalls outside, waiting to be butchered, and their lowing and squealing was the only thing to break the silence.

Getting ready to leave, Maria called him over to a table outside the back door. She held a large piece of thin metal up to the light.

"He drew crosses on this and then cut them out with those snippers. I think that solves part of the mystery. The only thing else is why?"

"If he's our man, which I doubt, he must have worked on this for years." He took the flat sheet of metal and held it up to the light. "See? Only two crosses missing, and those are in his pocket. Seems handy."

"Another setup?"

"That's my guess, or it could be a fresh sheet. But why have the butcher try to kill me? Why doesn't Ox do it himself?"

"You don't know the man. It's all about the game, moving the pieces around. Manipulating people."

She paused a moment. "Maybe he was supposed to incapacitate you. Make you helpless. Then Oxford could step in. That seems more like him."

"You seem to have made a study of him."

"Like I'd study a snake to see how far it could strike."

They walked out into the evening air. Standing upwind of the stench, it was good to take a clean breath. Only the slight smell of gunpowder marred the evening, and a creaking wagon bearing the body of the butcher.

Coble's voice carried soft over the breeze. "You always wondered more about the why of things."

She leaned against his arm. "And you just want to know who—so you can stop it."

"You know my rule. It's not what you say, it's what you do that defines a person."

He wasn't surprised when she took his hand.

Her voice was soft. "Can't we leave? There's nothing for us here but death."

A promise made to a grieving mother and himself came to his mind as he shook his head.

"Trying to protect him?"

Light shimmered off her hair as she shook her head. "To save us. No more."

His questions changed direction, looking back at the building. "Did you notice anything peculiar at the butcher's place?"

Shrugging, she shook her head again, recognizing the dismissal. "Hangs meat, stinks, cuts little crosses out of metal. What could be peculiar?"

"No rifle. No pistol. He killed livestock with a sap or stunned them so he could cut their throat. We still don't know who killed Billy Baker or those men a year ago. If this butcher, having no guns, is another man hired to take me down, and your dandy doesn't use a rifle—"

It always came down to that simple choice, when you throw out the complications. He shivered, thinking of all those old sayings of someone walking on your grave. He put a brave front on about not caring if he died, but the truth of it? He wasn't ready. There was work to do.

They hung Fred's lantern on the livery door and moved back toward his office. She stepped close as the night drew down and the wind whipped dust in the street. Thunder rumbled in the distance, and the smell of rain was fresh and inviting, replacing the stench they'd left moments before.

She tried again. "Can't we leave, Coble? What's left? Maybe this man was the killer. We'll never know."

"It doesn't fit, and you know it. The butcher was a pawn lacking the finesse for the rest of it. And your man has a habit of getting other people to do his work. Besides, he's confessed to you. Has he not?"

"Not my man."

He tried to push down the rising anger. "That's what your comment is for all this? He's not your man?"

"It's the most important part."

"You say that, but it seems you left me for him with little provocation. Can you answer that?"

"I'm sorry about that and about my temper. I told you why. All of it. Coble, we don't need a fancy piece of paper. You can have me when you want. Anytime. Anywhere. I'll be around. Marriage or not. I know you don't trust me. But you'll still have me. I'll prove myself."

Her burning fingers stroked the back of his neck. He wouldn't give her the satisfaction of turning to her, though his soul cried for it. Lack of trust is the worst casualty of something like this.

When he didn't respond, she continued. "I don't understand."

"I know. You never have." He sighed and watched her a moment. "I never wanted to love you. But I did. And that spell you cast made me want things I'd never considered before. Unreasonable as it sounds I wanted a home, a family, a sedate life. I dreamed of doing my job and always coming back to you. You spoke once of children. I dreamed of them. A little boy. A little girl. In my dreams, I could see them perfectly. I still dream of them. But they're toddlers. They've never grown. They never will because they'll never be born. They're ghosts of a life that I'll never have."

"That's not who we are, Coble. I'd like that, too. But life won't let us. We'd be running off to catch a killer when we should be home."

The darkness was a shroud keeping him from reading her face.

"You lied to me."

Her hands dropped as she took a quick breath. She tried to move away, but he caught her arm.

"I'm sorry." Her anguished voice broke. "I was trying to get us out of this town. Away from Oxford. But don't be hypocritical, Coble. You're no saint."

"It's not what you did with him that eats at me, although it's bad enough. It's the lie you gave while trying to win me over. It's hard to separate fact from unlikely choices."

Her figure was a vague outline as she moved away, heels clicking on the wooden planks.

"Maria. Wait."

"Walk with me to see Mrs. Peabody. You two seem to have a lot in common. Maybe we can figure something out and put an end to this."

Chapter Fourteen

THE WALK TO KATE'S HOUSE COULDN'T HAVE BEEN more somber had it been a funeral march. Neither spoke as they approached. A light burned inside the front entrance, the other windows were dark.

Coble stopped at the front door. Unlatched, it moved inward with a shove from the toe of his boot. He stepped inside, blocking Maria from coming in.

Kate was home. He could see her lying in the middle of the floor, among the shattered remains of a ladder-back chair. The inside of the room was in shambles, with blood splattered on the walls. Furniture lay overturned and a chair was in pieces, looking like something large fell on it.

Undisturbed, a coal-oil lantern rested on a table close to the front window. Palming his pistol while moving into the room, Coble took the lantern to check on Kate.

There was little to recognize of her face, but it

was enough. The awkward angle of her neck and back gave him a picture of her last moments. She looked like a rag doll thrown to the floor. He stayed kneeling with his hand on her shoulder, remembering her laughing eyes, her smell, her taste.

Had she cried for help with no one to save her? His hand trembled as he said a short prayer for her soul—and his.

A gasp from behind told him Maria had come inside. "Oh, my god."

He checked all the rooms, but her assailant was long gone. Stopping in her bedroom, he noticed the bedclothes had blood on them. Maybe the fight started there—and there was a fight.

"Who could have done this?"

"After all the killing going on, you have to ask?"

She looked around. "But this? Oxford isn't this strong. Someone was really angry."

He shrugged. "Or fighting hard." He couldn't decide if his churning stomach was from sadness or anger.

Maria looked around. "Whoever did this lost control. There's a wildness here we've not seen before. Like a wild animal caught in a cage."

Coble sat the lantern back on the table. Turning away, a bullet came searching through the window. The sound of the shot came at the same time as the results, as the lantern flew off the table, spreading fire that took root on the wood floor.

The front door was suicide. Grabbing Maria by the hand, he led her through the room to a back window. Pulling her through, he jumped to the side into the darkness next to the wall. The shooter must have guessed his intent. A bullet slammed into the wall just as they left.

If they were bait, the trap was set in haste because they were able to keep to the shadows and make their way back to the street and the stable. Both were breathing hard as they ran into the building.

Fred popped out of a back room. "What's going on? What's all the shooting?"

Maria explained while Coble stood watch by the door. People were shouting and running toward the house, but there wasn't much hope for saving the structure or the body inside.

"We've been played again."

They stood inside the doors, encased in shadow. "The lantern was left by the window for an easy shot. When I replaced it, the killer took advantage. Probably hoping we'd have oil splattered all over us from the lantern. As it is, he still almost got us. That fire spread fast."

The hostler spoke up. "What about Mrs. Peabody?"

"She was already dead. Beaten and cut up." He turned to Maria again. "There was a rug right next to the table the lantern was on, along with that crumbled chair. It was kindling."

"Why wouldn't he just burn it?"

"I'm betting he was going to. With a fire, everyone would think Kate perished from that, not from a beating. Fire is a common enough occurrence. No, someone waited to see if we'd show up."

"What now?"

"Now? We get Oxford Graham."

"You're too late." Fred's face reflected the fire a quarter-mile away. "I saw him in a buggy an hour or so ago, headed east toward Joplin. Had three men riding with him and they looked mean."

"I've met them."

He and Maria exchanged glances. She nodded. "He hired them just before you killed Sanibel. They showed up too late to help box you in."

"Your hand in your purse—a pistol?"

"If it came to that."

"I know you were surprised when I came in. If you were willing to kill him once the shooting started, why haven't you done it before now?"

Her gaze held steady on him. "Same reason as you. All I'd heard were subtle inferences of what he'd done. That's how he gets away with everything. He manipulates people into doing what he wants."

"Coble?" She continued in a soft voice. "If Oxford is gone, who shot in the window and started the fire?"

"Exactly."

———

THEY TIED their horses to the rail in front of Jack's Palace in Joplin, Missouri. Instead of following right away, they'd rested and left Hard

Times a little after dawn. They didn't push their horses and arrived before noon. The ten miles was easy riding.

The ending would come in this wide-open mining town. Oxford Graham would not be hiding this time. His pieces in place, and with three men to back him up, the man would be ready.

Maria had changed into range clothes, but no one would mistake her for a man. The contrast of her in the green-silk dress at the dance and her hard-bitten-down look now made him shake his head.

As they stood by their horses, a man approached from across the street. Looking past him, Coble saw he'd come out of the town marshal's office.

"I'm LC Hamilton, town marshal. Might I ask what you folks are doing in town?"

"My wife and I"—he cut a glance at Maria's smirk—"are in town to look up an acquaintance. How does that concern you?"

"Look. I know who you are, Mr. Bray. Word is you're persecuting a man because he had dealings with your wife. He and three others said it was consensual. I don't want any trouble."

Coble looked around as a fist-fight erupted in the street between two freight wagons while another stood on the wagon, lashing them with a long whip. Shots echoed from farther up the street, and a woman screamed. Between the dogs barking and people yelling, it took a moment to form a reply.

"And what would you classify as trouble? This place is coming apart at the seams."

The man shrugged. "This is normal trouble. You're extra."

Maria stepped up. "Since you've already been warned of our arrival, perhaps you can tell us where to find Oxford Graham?"

"Just because—"

"Marshal? The man you're protecting is guilty of the murder of several men and women, not to mention a Federal Judge in Kansas City."

"You got a warrant for all that?"

Coble looked at him a moment, not liking what he saw and reminding him of the man they wanted —too slick to pin down and well-versed in side-stepping.

Anger colored his voice. "Trot him out, LC. Then you can go back to whatever it is you do around here."

"Alright. Fine. He's right here in the Palace." He pointed at the double doors behind them. "The man's having lunch in the restaurant with his friends."

It was a big building and he stood gazing at the upper balcony. "Is that on the first floor? What else is in there?"

LC Hamilton sighed, giving the impression he wanted to leave. "The second floor is the gambling hall. The third floor is the bordello."

Coble laughed. "Bordello?"

"Whore house." Maria's voice had an edge to it. "You get up there much, LC?"

"Not that it's any of your business, but yes. All the ladies have to pay a fee to the city, or they get closed down." He tipped his hat to them. "If I close them down, the miners would burn the city to the ground. Nevertheless, it's a thriving economy."

They watched the man as he retreated to his office, dodging wagons and horses.

———

THE FIRST-FLOOR RESTAURANT was a study of opulence, with a padded staircase on the side leading upstairs. A polished dark-wood bar ran along one wall, but no boots had ever marred the shine of the brass footrail attached to the bottom. A bartender served the waiters, taking drinks to the patrons. A bat-wing door at the back of the room led to a kitchen. The muted rattle of pots and pans was the only testament to work done in the background.

They found the foursome sitting at a corner table in high-backed, plush chairs framed by tall plants.

Not giving them a chance to react, Coble's voice rapped out. "You men put your pistols on the table —real slow. I'm in no hurry."

Coble hadn't drawn his pistol, but they could see Maria pointing a shotgun at their table.

Her voice was soft and reasonable, with a

musical lilt from her Mexican heritage. "I'm taking up slack. Coble says this gun will put a bruise on my shoulder. If it does, I'm thinking you won't be around to see the results."

Guns clattered on the table, along with cuss words and disgusted looks.

Coble spoke again. "Alright, you three gents get up and stand over there by that...whatever bush that is. Anything else? Knives? Hide-out guns? I'm going to be real upset if you don't give them up now."

A couple of smaller pistols came out, along with a derringer. All deposited on the table.

Ox watched with wide eyes and finally found his voice. "What are you men doing? You're supposed to kill these people, not give up."

One of the men spoke. "Mister, we haven't seen the color of your money yet. And we're kind of boxed in here. I'm thinking we'll call it a day and hit the trail—if that's alright with the marshal and his lady?"

"You're not the one we want, so take off."

After watching them walk away, Coble brought his attention the Oxford. "Now, Ox—"

"Stop." Maria moved up to the table, still holding the shotgun on the man. "Your sleeve gun. Point your right arm away from us and take it out. Don't test me, Oxford. All I need is an excuse."

Coble pulled the table full of pistols away from the man. "Now stand up."

A quick check found no other weapons except for a leather sap stuck in his back pocket.

"Know what's better than shooting this man, Maria? He's going to hang. All his plotting and scheming won't get him out of it. I'll talk to the trapdoor artist and make sure it's a short drop with a bad knot. Probably take several minutes to stretch his neck out. I don't usually attend hangings, but I'll attend this one."

When she didn't answer, he looked over his shoulder. Maria was big-eyed, and Faraday held her shotgun.

He stared at the man a moment. "I thought you were headed to Kansas City?"

"Telegraph caught me at the rails, sent me to Joplin instead."

"So, why all this? Money?"

"Ain't it always?" Faraday shrugged. "Got some gambling debts. This seemed the quickest way out of hock."

"You're backing the wrong horse and it could get you dead. You must know this will not end well."

"Maybe. Maybe not. We're not having a convention of saints here."

Coble turned back to a smiling Oxford Graham. "Why? Why all this, Ox? Why the games?"

"Where's the fun? Marshal Bray, you kill and take no pleasure in it at all. Anyone can be a plain old killer like you. That's easy. Games make it fun."

"Why me?" He pointed at Maria. "Why her?"

He sat calm in his chair, a serene smile stretching his face. "You might recall a minister down in Big Springs? He was my brother."

"I remember a little weasel who murdered innocent girls. Finias Stone. And I didn't kill him."

"No. Not directly. But I know you arranged it and gave him over to those savages. So, I arranged this. Kind of tit for tat."

Oxford straightened his coat lapels. "I couldn't believe it. I tried to get you to play once before, when those thieves died at your feet. I even left you a note, but you just rode on your merry way and wound up killing my brother. If you'd played the game, he'd be alive."

He looked around at them. "So here we are. Even at the end, you believe I've been out-maneuvered. Surprise! You can't outthink me, Mr. Bray."

Coble glanced around at curious patrons watching from tables, a waiter standing a few feet away. "So you're going to kill us? Right here?"

"You think the marshal will intervene? Or anyone? Do you think a whore house and gambling hall would be built right across the street from an honest town marshal?"

"I don't know." He smiled and shrugged. "I have my gun, so you're dead either way. Faraday won't shoot me in the back, neither will he shoot a defenseless woman. It's not in him."

"If you draw your weapon, he'll kill her. You won't take that chance. Besides, he won't have to kill you. I'll do it with pleasure." Oxford's expression turned into a mask of fury—and then slack-jawed surprise.

Coble turned to see Priest holding a gun on

Faraday. Maria had her shotgun back, pointing at Oxford.

He took a deep, relieved breath. "This is starting to resemble a comedy. What are you doing here, Priest?"

"Oh, I just got off the train and came in for a bite to eat." He gazed past Coble. "Do you believe this is the man responsible for killing Jenny?"

"And a few others."

"He doesn't seem like much. The devil seems to be hiding in a cheap suit and cowardly little man. Leave him with me and I'll take care of him, if you don't mind."

"Sorry. Much as I'd like to, I've got my heart set on watching him hang. It's a better way, Priest. Didn't you mention worrying about becoming what we were fighting against? We'll take him back to Kansas City."

"Seems a monumental waste of time and energy considering the newspapers, politicians, and jack-leg lawyers that will flock to this. But I'll bow to your wisdom."

"I'm surprised Juana let you make this trip."

Priest chuckled. "I bribed her. She's looking for a wedding dress."

Coble took out the bag of trinkets and rattled them at Oxford. "I have to return these remembrances to you, but I'm having trouble deciding where to put them. I can't tell if they'd be better served in your grave or on my mantle."

They stood him up and tied his hands with a

leather strap. "You're being rather docile for a man on the way to a hanging, Ox."

"I'll have my way, sooner or later. The game's not over." He smiled at them, trying to catch each one's attention. "It may be just starting."

"Well, I disagree. I think your three hired guns are long gone and Faraday does not seem too committed to your cause once he found out the reputation of his employer. What else can you come up with? Do you have more surprises set up?"

A waiter came up and asked what to do with all the guns. "Keep them, sell them, turn them in to the city marshal. I don't care. Maybe you can get the price of their meal from it."

Maria went out the door first, along with Priest and Faraday. When Priest turned and nodded, he pushed Graham out into the crowded walkway.

They weren't expecting the final surprise. They heard the melon-strike of a bullet hitting Oxford in the head and the thump of the round hitting the wall beyond before the sound of a shot came to them. Oxford slumped, and a man just beyond him yelped in pain, looking at his bloody arm and the gouge in the wood. When he wiped the blood spray from his face, he turned and threw up over a hitching rail. Since that was a daily occurrence in a hard-drinking town, few people gave him any notice.

Still standing in the protection of the doorway, Coble stood straight as people shied away and ducked for cover. He was looking at the row of buildings down the street. Against the backdrop of a smelter in the distance, trailing smoke and steam into the air, there was little hope of seeing where the bullet came from.

When no other shots came, Faraday stood up, looked at the carnage once called Oxford Graham, and faced Coble. "What are you going to do with me?"

Coble shrugged, pulling his gaze from the buildings. "As I see it, your only crime was stupidity, and you didn't carry it through. It's a fault I often find in myself. Talk to the town marshal. Tell him what you know before you leave. Write it down for him and sign it. He may have a short memory."

He offered his hand to the man, holding his gaze. "Don't let me catch you on my back trail, if you don't mind."

LC Hamilton shouldered his way through the crowd. "I told you—"

Coble clasped the man on the shoulder. "Just the man I need. You've several deputies? Good. Check those rooftops toward the end of the street for a rifle left there. Maybe a Sharps or Whitworth."

Priest came to stand by him. "What are you thinking?"

He looked at his friend and then at the tired face of Maria. The squeal of ungreased wheels on freight wagons, yelling teamsters, and the whistle of steam from the smelter signifying a shift change could not cover the discordant and pounding litany of ivory keys in a building a few doors down the street. And it just started.

He gave a small, grim nod of satisfaction. "Why, like the Pied Piper of old, I'm going to follow the music."

————

THE BUILDING HAD a bar crowded with a melting pot of men wearing buckskin to miner's hats, stretching the length of one wall, with a door open in the back supplying poor ventilation. Beer and whiskey flowed as smooth as the soiled doves flitting around. There was scant room between the tables for walking. The piano was in the back, close to the door, and angled so the soundboard faced the patrons. With no hesitation in his nimble fingers, the piano man watched them approach.

Coble watched him play a moment before dropping his gaze to the man's hands—hands that showed cuts and bruising, some still seeping blood.

"Must be painful." The playing stopped a moment as the man raised his eyebrows in question. "You should get those hands looked at."

Not trying to hide them, the man rubbed blood from his knuckle. "They'll heal."

Up to now, this had been a hunch, a gut feeling. Now, he was sure. "It was your undoing, you know."

His fingers caressed the keys, playing a silent tune and leaving bloody streaks. "I don't know what you mean?"

"When you beat Kate Peabody to death. And then shot through the lamp to start the fire and try to burn us. That was your discordant note that I talked to your partner about. He must have told you. The only question is why?"

One of his fingers pressed down, playing one note. It was gradually becoming a room full of whispers as people watched. Priest and Maria turned and faced the crowd.

His gaze took in the crowd and then settled on Coble. "This piano needs to be tuned."

"I asked you a question."

The man looked at Coble with an intent gaze. "To answer would be an admission, would it not?"

"The admission is in your bloody hands, the mud on your boots, and the fresh tracks coming in this open doorway leading to your feet. From the powder sprinkled around your eyes, I'm guessing Marshal Hamilton will find an old rifle on a rooftop. Not the great distance you're used to, but a pretty fair shot."

Priest moved up beside him, pointing a pistol at the piano man. "LC is coming in the front door."

A panting voice came from the marshal. "We found a rifle on the roof above Ziler's Mercantile."

"An old Whitworth?"

Before he could answer, another man with a deputy's badge pinned on his vest stepped through the back door, looked at the muddy tracks and the piano man's boots, and then nodded to the town marshal.

The deputy's voice was hoarse. "They've been pumping water from an old tunnel. I trailed him from Ziler's to here."

Coble nodded, still watching the piano man. "Marshal Hamilton, do you know the reputation of that old rifle having a lot of blow-back?"

"I do. It was used a lot in the late war."

He looked at the man sitting on the piano bench. "Well, piano man. It seems we don't need an admission at all. But I would like an answer or two. It would be a kindness for people concerned."

Dead eyes stared back at him as the man shrugged.

"How'd you know Oxford Graham?"

His expressionless face looked at them. "Met during the war. We worked some jobs together. He'd spot and I'd shoot."

"I'm guessing he supplied opium in sufficient quantities to settle your nerves and give you a steady hand?"

The man nodded.

"Why kill him?"

"I knew he'd fold and give me up." He glanced again at the people surrounding him. "And I grew tired of his games."

"And Mrs. Peabody?"

He looked away toward the opening of the back door. "I am sorry about that one. My temper has been hard to control lately. Oxford said the woman was wanting to talk to you and knew too much. She was getting too close."

To be beat to death is a long and ugly way to die. Kate Peabody had wanted one thing. The killer of her young husband found and punished—killed if she had her way. He wished she knew...maybe she did.

"And Billy Baker? He was a young man, full of life. One of the best horsemen I've seen. His mother is alone now. How can that be justified?"

The man stared a moment, looking at the ceiling and back to the keyboard. "More games to get your attention. He wanted you to feel impotent and make people not respect you when you couldn't solve the killings."

Coble shook his head. "All he got from me was anger. Did Oxford Graham actually kill anyone or just order it done?"

"He did. He got the easy ones. That German farmer." He looked at Priest. "Your woman. I think that one bothered him a little."

Coble shrugged a moment, trying to bolster tired legs and a jaded mind. A brown arm gripped him around his waist as Maria broke in.

"What about Judge MacGregor? Did he admit to that?"

The piano man smiled at her. "I've no idea. Oxford killed for pleasure and should have killed you first thing. You were nothing but trouble waiting to happen." His gaze slipped to Coble. "I killed for need, nothing more. And it keeps getting worse."

Oxford must have been a master if he got his

sharpshooter hooked on opium and then supplied his need to make the man do his bidding.

"You got a name?"

He played a few notes with one hand. "I'm nobody." The vacant stare was back again, along with a small smile. "Piano man will do."

Coble watched him a moment. A monster sat before him, revealed behind the dead, flat eyes waiting for release. It would take a long time to forget those eyes. How could a blank stare show so much? And bring such fear.

"LC, if you'll take this man into custody, I'll sign the papers." He looked around the room full of patrons and deputies. "I'm sure there are enough witnesses to make your case to a judge. And Marshal?"

He turned and made sure he had the man's attention. "You be real careful around this man."

———

IT WAS a quiet ride back to Hard Times and was near dark when they gathered in front of Fred's livery and explained everything to Fred and Tom Fallon.

"So, it's over?" Tom took off his hat and combed his hair with his fingers. "I can give this job up? Do something else?"

Fred was watching him. "Are you staying, Coble? We talked about this. How many died? There's—"

"I don't need a list, Fred."

Coble watched Priest walking across the street toward the sheriff's office and an impatient-looking Juana.

"You've done a good job, Tom. Keep the town clean and you may get a church and school. The saloons aren't something that will last much longer."

Fred snorted. "Doubt that'll ever happen." He paused a moment. "What's next for you, Coble? What will you do? You're a good man, but you're a damned lightning rod for trouble."

What was next? He was tired, and Maria hadn't moved from his side. According to her, it's where she belonged. Maybe in time? Trust is a commodity easily lost and hard to regain. He shook his head, trying to clear the cobwebs.

In a few months, this town would be little more than a dusty street with a ventilated windmill in the center. The general store and eatery would survive. There was nothing else of value for longevity, unless they could get good people to put down roots.

He'd looked for one killer and found an unholy trinity preying on innocents. A cold knot settled in his belly, and his hand rested on the butt of his pistol, sweat-stained and worn smooth. A tool? Or a curse?

"Well, Fred. There's a man waiting at the ranch to speak to his daughter. If I don't bring her back, my life isn't worth a plugged nickel. Whether I'm going home is a question without an answer."

Maria turned him to face her. "It will be a home. We got things backward, you and me. We should have told our secrets before the marriage, not after. We've made mistakes, but if you think of our marriage as a house, we've a good foundation, and the center will hold against the wind."

Fred cleared his throat. "That's all fine and good. I wish you all the luck in the world." He hesitated a moment. "But there's one more little problem."

He backed up a step when they turned to face him.

"You owe me a dollar a day...and your paint ain't worth all that much."

A Look at Book Three:
The Murder Book

In the shadowy depths of turbulent history, one weary lawman faces his most daunting challenge yet.

When a cold-blooded murderer escapes from jail, Deputy U.S. Marshal Coble Bray hunts him down to the organized crime syndicate of Joplin, Missouri—a town as wild as Tombstone, where corruption runs deep.

As Coble navigates a treacherous web of criminals, city officials, and a compromised law enforcement system, he grows weary of the endless violence and chaos that define his life. With his federal warrant suddenly revoked, he can't help but contemplate retirement, yearning for a semblance of normalcy.

But when the fight comes to him—putting everything he loves on the line—Coble vows that evil has underestimated the fire it ignites for the last time. And he's about to burn it all to ash.

Will Coble Bray be extinguished by the chaos, or will he finally close the book on murder?

AVAILABLE NOVEMBER 2024

About the Author

Darrel Sparkman is an award-winning author of novels, novellas, and short stories. He's been included in three western anthologies, worked as a feature writer for *Saddlebag Dispatches* and blogged a short time for *Sundown Press*.

His ideas come from a diverse past of serving as a combat search and rescue helicopter crewman in Vietnam and volunteer Emergency Medical Technician First Responder. He has worked as a professional photographer, computer repair tech, and was once part-owner of a commercial greenhouse operation and flower shop.

Darrel is enjoying semi-retirement and finally has that job that wakes him up every day—with a smile on his face.